EVERYMAN,
I WILL GO WITH THEE
AND BE THY GUIDE,
IN THY MOST NEED
TO GO BY THY SIDE

POEMS OF
SLEEP AND
DREAMS

EVERYMAN'S LIBRARY
POCKET POETS

Alfred A. Knopf New York London Toronto

THIS IS A BORZOI BOOK

PUBLISHED BY ALFRED A. KNOPF

This selection by Peter Washington first published in
Everyman's Library, 2004
Copyright © 2004 by Everyman's Library

A list of acknowledgments to copyright owners appears at the back
of this volume.

All rights reserved under International and Pan-American Copyright
Conventions. Published in the United States by Alfred A. Knopf, a
division of Random House, Inc., New York, and simultaneously in
Canada by Random House of Canada Limited, Toronto. Distributed by
Random House, Inc., New York. Published in the United Kingdom by
Everyman's Library, Northburgh House, 10 Northburgh Street, London
EC1V 0AT. Distributed by Random House (UK) Ltd.

US website: www.randomhouse.com/everymans

ISBN 1-4000-4197-X (US)
1-84159-760-0 (UK)

A CIP catalogue record for this book is available from the British Library

Library of Congress Cataloging-in-Publication Data
Poems of sleep and dreams / selected and edited by Peter Washington.
p. cm.—(Everyman's Library pocket poets)
"A Borzoi book."
ISBN 1-4000-4197-X (alk. paper)
1. Sleep—Poetry. 2. Dreams—Poetry. I. Washington, Peter. II. Series.
PN6110.S55P64 2004   2003064218
808.81'9353—dc22

Typography by Peter B. Willberg

Typeset in the UK by AccComputing, North Barrow, Somerset

Printed and bound in Germany by GGP Media, Pössneck

CONTENTS

SLEEP

SLEEPERS

6

THE NEAREST DREAM

NIGHTMARES

THE INTERPRETATION OF DREAMS

INSOMNIA

Now I will tell you how the waves of quiet
Flow through the mind in sleep and release it from care;
I will make the verses sweet and not too many
For the swan's little song is better than all the clamour
Of cranes blowing about in the clouds from the south.

from Lucretius, De Rerum Natura IV,
translated by C. H. Sisson

NOCTURNAL

HYMN TO CYNTHIA

Queen and huntress, chaste and fair,
Now the sun is laid to sleep,
Seated in thy silver chair,
State in wonted manner keep:
   Hesperus entreats thy light,
   Goddess excellently bright.

Earth, let not thy envious shade
Dare itself to interpose;
Cynthia's shining orb was made
Heaven to clear, when day did close:
   Bless us then with wishèd sight,
   Goddess excellently bright.

Lay thy bow of pearl apart,
And thy crystal-shining quiver;
Give unto the flying hart
Space to breathe, how short soever:
   Thou that mak'st a day of night,
   Goddess excellently bright.

BEN JONSON (1572–1637)

BEFORE SLEEP

The toil of day is ebbing,
  The quiet comes again,
In slumber deep relaxing
  The limbs of tired men.

And minds with anguish shaken,
  And spirits racked with grief,
The cup of all forgetting
  Have drunk and found relief.

The still Lethean waters
  Now steal through every vein,
And men no more remember
  The meaning of their pain. . . .

Let, let the weary body
  Lie sunk in slumber deep.
The heart shall still remember
  Christ in its very sleep.

18 PRUDENTIUS(384–410)
      TRANSLATED BY HELEN WADDELL

EVENING QUATRAINS

The day's grown old, the fainting sun
Has but a little way to run,
And yet his steeds, with all his skill,
Scarce lug the chariot down the hill.

With labour spent, and thirst opprest,
Whilst they strain hard to gain the West,
From fetlocks hot drops melted light,
Which turn to meteors in the night.

The shadows now so long do grow,
That brambles like tall cedars show,
Mole-hills seem mountains, and the ant
Appears a monstrous elephant.

A very little, little flock
Shades thrice the ground that it would stock;
Whilst the small stripling following them,
Appears a mighty Polypheme.

These being brought into the fold,
And by the thrifty master told,
He thinks his wages are well paid,
Since none are either lost, or stray'd.

Now lowing herds are each-where heard,
Chains rattle in the villain's yard,
The cart's on tail set down to rest,
Bearing on high the Cuckold's crest.

The hedge is stripped, the clothes brought in,
Nought's left without should be within,
The bees are hiv'd, and hum their charm,
Whilst every house does seem a swarm.

The cock now to the roost is prest;
For he must call up all the rest;
The sow's fast pegg'd within the sty,
To still her squeaking progeny.

Each one has had his supping mess,
The cheese is put into the press,
The pans and bowls clean scalded all,
Rear'd up against the milk-house wall.

And now on benches all are sat
In the cool air to sit and chat,
Till Phœbus, dipping in the West,
Shall lead the world the way to rest.

EVENING VOLUNTARIES (I)

Calm is the fragrant air, and loth to lose
Day's grateful warmth, tho' moist with falling dews.
Look for the stars, you'll say that there are none;
Look up a second time, and, one by one,
You mark them twinkling out with silvery light,
And wonder how they could elude the sight!
The birds, of late so noisy in their bowers,
Warbled a while with faint and fainter powers,
But now are silent as the dim-seen flowers:
Nor does the village Church-clock's iron tone
The time's and season's influence disown;
Nine beats distinctly to each other bound
In drowsy sequence – how unlike the sound
That, in rough winter, oft inflicts a fear
On fireside listeners, doubting what they hear!
The shepherd, bent on rising with the sun,
Had closed his door before the day was done,
And now with thankful heart to bed doth creep,
And joins his little children in their sleep.
The bat, lured forth where trees the lane o'ershade,
Flits and reflits along the close arcade;
The busy dor-hawk chases the white moth
With burring note, which Industry and Sloth
Might both be pleased with, for it suits them both.
A stream is heard – I see it not, but know

By its soft music whence the waters flow:
Wheels and the tread of hoofs are heard no more;
One boat there was, but it will touch the shore
With the next dipping of its slackened oar;
Faint sound, that, for the gayest of the gay,
Might give to serious thought a moment's sway,
As a last token of man's toilsome day!

NODDING

Tizdal my beautiful cat
Lies on the old rag mat
In front of the kitchen fire.
Outside the night is black.

The great fat cat
Lies with his paws under him
His whiskers twitch in a dream,
He is slumbering.

The clock on the mantelpiece
Ticks unevenly, tic toc, tic-toc,
Good heavens what is the matter
With the kitchen clock?

Outside an owl hunts,
Hee hee hee hee,
Hunting in the Old Park
From his snowy tree.
What on earth can he find in the park tonight,
It is so wintry?

Now the fire burns suddenly too hot
Tizdal gets up to move,
Why should such an animal
Provoke our love?

The twigs from the elder bush
Are tapping on the window pane
As the wind sets them tapping,
Now the tapping begins again.

One laughs on a night like this
In a room half firelight half dark
With a great lump of a cat
Moving on the hearth,
And the twigs tapping quick,
And the owl in an absolute fit.
One laughs supposing creation
Pays for its long plodding
Simply by coming to this –
Cat, night, fire – and a girl nodding.

A NOCTURNAL SKETCH

Even is come; and from the dark Park, hark,
The signal of the setting sun – one gun!
And six is sounding from the chime, prime time
To go and see the Drury-Lane Dane slain, –

Or hear Othello's jealous doubt spout out, –
Or Macbeth raving at that shade-made blade,
Denying to his frantic clutch much touch; –
Or else to see Ducrow with wide stride ride
Four horses as no other man can span;
Or in the small Olympic Pit, sit split
Laughing at Liston, while you quiz his phiz.

Anon Night comes, and with her wings brings things
Such as, with his poetic tongue, Young sung;
The gas up-blazes with its bright white light,
And paralytic watchmen prowl, howl, growl,
About the streets and take up Pall-Mall Sal,
Who, hasting to her nightly jobs, robs, fobs.

Now thieves to enter for your cash, smash, crash,
Past drowsy Charley in a deep sleep, creep,
But frightened by Policeman B.3, flee,
And while they're going, whisper low, 'No go!'

Now puss, while folks are in their beds, treads leads,
And sleepers waking, grumble –, 'Drat that cat!'
Who in the gutter caterwauls, squalls, mauls
Some feline foe, and screams in shrill ill-will.

Now Bulls of Bashan, and of prize size, rise
In childish dreams, and with a roar gore poor
Georgy, or Charley, or Billy, willy-nilly; –
But Nursemaid in a nightmare rest, chest-pressed,
Dreameth of one of her old flames, James Games,
And that she hears – what faith is man's – Ann's banns
And his, from Reverend Mr. Rice, twice, thrice:
White ribbons flourish, and a stout shout out,
That upward goes, shows Rose knows those
        bows' woes.

WINTER NIGHT

Snow, snow, all the world over,
Snow to the world's end swirling,
A candle was burning on the table,
A candle burning.

As midges swarming in summer
Fly to the candle flame,
The snowflakes swarming outside
Flew at the window frame.

The blizzard etched on the window
Frosty patterning.
A candle was burning on the table,
A candle burning.

The lighted ceiling carried
A shadow frieze:
Entwining hands, entwining feet,
Entwining destinies.

And two little shoes dropped,
Thud, from the mattress.
And candle wax like tears dropped
On an empty dress.

And all was lost in a tunnel
Of grey snow churning.
A candle was burning on the table,
A candle burning.

And when a draught flattened the flame,
Temptation blazed
And like a fiery angel raised
Two cross-shaped wings.

All February the snow fell
And sometimes till morning
A candle was burning on the table,
A candle burning.

28   BORIS PASTERNAK (1890–1960)
TRANSLATED BY JON STALLWORTHY AND
PETER FRANCE

SONNET TO THE MOON

Now every leaf, though colorless, burns bright
With disembodied and celestial light,
And drops without a movement or a sound
A pillar of darkness to the shifting ground.

The lucent, thin, and alcoholic flame
Runs in the stubble with a nervous aim,
But, when the eye pursues, will point with fire
Each single stubble-tip and strain no higher.

O triple goddess! Contemplate my plight!
Opacity, my fate! Change, my delight!
The yellow tom-cat, sunk in shifting fur,
Changes and dreams, a phosphorescent blur.

Sullen I wait, but still the vision shun.
Bodiless thoughts and thoughtless bodies run.

YVOR WINTERS (1900–68)   29

THE NIGHT PIECE

The fog drifts slowly down the hill
And as I mount gets thicker still,
Closes me in, makes me its own
Like bedclothes on the paving stone.

Here are the last few streets to climb,
Galleries, run through veins of time,
Almost familiar, where I creep
Toward sleep like fog, through fog like sleep.

BERCEUSE

COME, SLEEP!

Come, Sleep! O Sleep, the certain knot of peace,
The baiting-place of wit, the balm of woe,
The poor man's wealth, the prisoner's release,
Th' indifferent judge between the high and low;
With shield of proof shield me from out the prease
Of those fierce darts Despair at me doth throw:
O make me in those civil wars to cease;
I will good tribute pay, if thou do so.
Take thou of me smooth pillows, sweetest bed,
A chamber deaf to noise and blind to light,
A rosy garland and a weary head:
And if these things, as being thine in right,
Move not thy heavy grace, thou shalt in me,
Livelier than elsewhere, Stella's image see.

PHILIP SIDNEY (1544–86)

GOOD NIGHT

In brilliant gas light
I turn the kitchen spigot
and watch the water plash
into the clean white sink.
On the grooved drain-board
to one side is
a glass filled with parsley –
crisped green.
                 Waiting
for the water to freshen –
I glance at the spotless floor –:
a pair of rubber sandals
lie side by side
under the wall-table
all is in order for the night.

Waiting, with a glass in my hand
– three girls in crimson satin
pass close before me on
the murmurous background of
the crowded opera –
                         it is

memory playing the clown –
three vague, meaningless girls
full of smells and
the rustling sound of
cloth rubbing on cloth and
little slippers on carpet –
high-school French
spoken in a loud voice!

Parsley in a glass,
still and shining,
brings me back. I take my drink
and yawn deliciously.
I am ready for bed.

LULLABY

Lay your sleeping head, my love,
Human on my faithless arm;
Time and fevers burn away
Individual beauty from
Thoughtful children, and the grave
Proves the child ephemeral:
But in my arms till break of day
Let the living creature lie,
Mortal, guilty, but to me
The entirely beautiful.

Soul and body have no bounds:
To lovers as they lie upon
Her tolerant enchanted slope
In their ordinary swoon,
Grave the vision Venus sends
Of supernatural sympathy,
Universal love and hope;
While an abstract insight wakes
Among the glaciers and the rocks
The hermit's carnal ecstasy.

Certainty, fidelity
On the stroke of midnight pass
Like vibrations of a bell
And fashionable madmen raise
Their pedantic boring cry:
Every farthing of the cost,
All the dreaded cards foretell,
Shall be paid, but from this night
Not a whisper, not a thought,
Not a kiss nor look be lost.

Beauty, midnight, vision dies:
Let the winds of dawn that blow
Softly round your dreaming head
Such a day of welcome show
Eye and knocking heart may bless,
Find our mortal world enough;
Noons of dryness find you fed
By the involuntary powers,
Nights of insult let you pass
Watched by every human love.

SLEEPE, ANGRY BEAUTY

Sleepe, angry beauty, sleep, and feare not me;
For who a sleeping Lyon dares provoke?
It shall suffice me here to sit and see
Those lips shut up that never kindely spoke.
    What sight can more content a lovers minde
    Than beauty seeming harmlesse, if not kinde?

My words have charm'd her, for secure shee sleepes,
Though guilty much of wrong done to my love;
And in her slumber, see, shee close-ey'd weepes;
Dreames often more than waking passions move.
    Pleade, sleepe, my cause, and make her soft like thee,
    That shee in peace may wake and pitty mee.

SLEEP, BABY MINE, DESIRE!

'Sleep, baby mine, Desire!' Nurse Beauty singeth.
'Thy cries, O baby, set mine head on aching.'
The babe cries 'Way, thy love doth keep me waking.'

'Lully, lully, my babe! Hope cradle bringeth
Unto my children always good rest taking.'
The babe cries 'Way, thy love doth me keep waking.'

'Since, baby mine, from me, thy watching springeth,
 Sleep then a little; pap Content is making:'
The babe cries 'Nay! for that abide I waking.'

PHILIP SIDNEY (1544–86)

AND SO TO BED

'Night-night, my Precious!'; '*Sweet* dreams, Sweet!'
'Heaven bless you, Child!' – the accustomed grown-ups
        said.
Two eyes gazed mutely back that none could meet,
Then turned to face Night's terrors overhead.

WALTER DE LA MARE (1873–1956)

DREAM WORLD

In your loving arms there lie
Serious field and fickle sky;
Syllables of your breath compose
Arctic wind and desert rose;
And fidgeting Atlantics sigh
To sleep beneath your lullaby.

Let the presaging planets weep.
No nightmares from their mirrors creep
To touch you with their breath and show
The eyes of innocence how to know
The world you dandle into sleep
Rocks your cradle six feet deep.

LULLABY

Sleep little baby, clean as a nut,
Your fingers uncurl and your eyes are shut.
Your life was ours, which is with you.
Go on your journey. We go too.

The bat is flying round the house
Like an umbrella turned into a mouse.
The moon is astonished and so are the sheep:
Their bells have come to send you to sleep.

Oh be our rest, our hopeful start.
Turn your head to my beating heart.
Sleep little baby, clean as a nut,
Your fingers uncurl and your eyes are shut.

BERCEUSE

Listen to Gieseking playing a Berceuse
of Chopin – the mothwing flutter
light as ash, perishable as burnt paper –

and sleep, now the furnaces of Auschwitz
are all out, and tourists go there.
The purest art has slept with turpitude,

we all pay taxes. Sleep. The day of waking
waits, cloned from the phoenix –
a thousand replicas in upright silos,

nurseries of the ultimate enterprise.
Decay will undo what it can, the rotten
fabric of our repose connives with doomsday.

Sleep on, scathed felicity. Sleep, rare
and perishable relic. Imagining's no shutter
against the absolute, incorrigible sunrise.

LULLABY

Beloved, may your sleep be sound
That have found it where you fed.
What were all the world's alarms
To mighty Paris when he found
Sleep upon a golden bed
That first dawn in Helen's arms?

Sleep, beloved, such a sleep
As did that wild Tristram know
When, the potion's work being done,
Roe could run or doe could leap
Under oak and beechen bough,
Roe could leap or doe could run;

Such a sleep and sound as fell
Upon Eurotas' grassy bank
When the holy bird, that there
Accomplished his predestined will,
From the limbs of Leda sank
But not from her protecting care.

W. B. YEATS (1865–1939) 43

A CRADLE SONG

Sleep, Sleep! beauty bright
Dreaming o'er the joys of night.
Sleep, Sleep! in thy sleep
Little sorrows sit & weep.

Sweet Babe, in thy face
Soft desires I can trace,
Secret joys & secret smiles,
Little pretty infant wiles.

As thy softest limbs I feel,
Smiles as of the morning steal
O'er thy cheek, & o'er thy breast
Where thy little heart does rest.

O! the cunning wiles that creep
In thy little heart asleep;
When thy little heart does wake
Then the dreadful lightnings break.

From thy cheek & from thy eye,
O'er the youthful harvests nigh,
Infant wiles & infant smiles
Heaven & Earth of peace beguiles.

SLEEP

TO SLEEP

O soft embalmer of the still midnight,
    Shutting, with careful fingers and benign,
Our gloom-pleas'd eyes, embower'd from the light,
    Enshaded in forgetfulness divine;
O soothest Sleep! if so it please thee, close,
    In midst of this thine hymn, my willing eyes,
Or wait the amen, ere thy poppy throws
    Around my bed its lulling charities;
    Then save me, or the passèd day will shine
Upon my pillow, breeding many woes;
    Save me from curious conscience, that still lords
Its strength for darkness, burrowing like a mole;
    Turn the key deftly in the oiled wards,
And seal the hushed casket of my soul.

CARE-CHARMER SLEEP

Care-charmer Sleep, son of the sable Night,
Brother to Death, in silent darkness born,
Relieve my languish, and restore the light;
With dark forgetting of my care return,
And let the day be time enough to mourn
The shipwreck of my ill-adventured youth:
Let waking eyes suffice to wail their scorn,
Without the torment of the night's untruth.
Cease, dreams, the images of day-desires,
To model forth the passions of the morrow;
Never let rising Sun approve you liars,
To add more grief to aggravate my sorrow:
    Still let me sleep, embracing clouds in vain,
    And never wake to feel the day's disdain.

SLEEP, SILENCE' CHILD

Sleep, Silence' child, sweet father of soft rest,
Prince whose approach peace to all mortals brings,
Indifferent host to shepherds and to kings,
Sole comforter of minds with grief opprest;
Lo, by thy charming-rod all breathing things
Lie slumbering, with forgetfulness possest,
And yet o'er me to spread thy drowsy wings
Thou spares, alas! who cannot be thy guest.
Since I am thine, O come, but with that face
To inward light which thou art wont to show;
With feignèd solace each a true-felt woe;
Or if, deaf god, thou do deny that grace,
Come as thou wilt, and what thou wilt bequeath, –
I long to kiss the image of my death.

IN SLEEP

The cries of owls, or the intermittent heartbeats
of dying butterflies,
or the moans and sighs
of the young, or the error that tightens
like a garrote around the temples, or the vague horror
of cedars uprooted by the onrush of night – all this
can come back to me, overflowing from ditches,
bursting from waterpipes, and awaken me
to your voice. The music of a slow, demented dance
cuts through; the enemy clangs down
his visor, hiding his face. The amaranth moon
enters behind the closed eyelids, becomes a swelling
cloud; and when sleep takes it
deeper in, it is still blood beyond any death.

50 EUGENIO MONTALE (1896–1981)
       TRANSLATED BY CHARLES WRIGHT

SLEEP IS SUPPOSED TO BE

Sleep is supposed to be
By souls of sanity
The shutting of the eye.

Sleep is the station grand
Down which, on either hand
The hosts of witness stand!

Morn is supposed to be
By people of degree
The breaking of the Day.

Morning has not occurred!

That shall Aurora be –
East of Eternity –
One with the banner gay –
One in the red array –
That is the break of Day!

EMILY DICKINSON (1830–86)

From METAMORPHOSES BOOK 11
THE CAVE OF SLEEP

Neere the *Cimmerians* lurks a Cave, in steepe
And hollow hills; the Mansion of dull *Sleepe*:
Not seene by *Phœbus* when he mounts the skies,
At height, nor stooping: gloomie mists arise
From humid earth, which still a twi-light make.
No crested fowles shrill crowings here awake
The chearefull Morne: no barking Sentinell
Here guards; nor geese, who wakefull dogs excell.
Beasts tame, nor salvage; no wind-shaken boughs,
Nor strife of jarring tongues, with noyses rouse
Securèd Ease. Yet from the rock a spring,
With streames of *Lethe* softly murmuring,
Purles on the pebbles, and invites Repose.
Before the Entry pregnant Poppie growes,
With numerous Simples; from whose juicie birth
Night gathers sleepe, and sheds it on the Earth.
No doores here on their creeking hinges jarr'd:
Through-out this court there was no doore, nor guard.
Amid the *Heben* cave a downie bed
High mounted stands, with sable coverings spred.
Here lay the lazie God, dissolv'd in rest.
Fantastick Dreames, who various formes exprest,
About him lay: then Autumn's eares far more;
Or leaves of trees, or sands on *Neptunes* shore.

TRANSLATED BY THOMAS SANDYS

MORPHEUS

Morpheus, the lively son of deadly sleep,
Witness of life to them that living die,
A prophet oft, and oft an history,
A poet eke, as humours fly or creep;
Since thou in me so sure a power dost keep,
That never I with closed-up sense do lie,
But by thy work my Stella I descry,
Teaching blind eyes both how to smile and weep;
Vouchsafe, of all acquaintance, this to tell,
Whence hast thou ivory, rubies, pearl, and gold,
To show her skin, lips, teeth, and head so well?
Fool! answers he; no Indes such treasures hold;
But from thy heart, while my sire charmeth thee,
Sweet Stella's image I do steal to me.

WALKING TO SLEEP

As a queen sits down, knowing that a chair will
    be there,
Or a general raises his hand and is given the
    field-glasses,
Step off assuredly into the blank of your mind.
Something will come to you. Although at first
You nod through nothing like a fogbound prow,
Gravel will breed in the margins of your gaze,
Perhaps with tussocks or a dusty flower,
And, humped like dolphins playing in the bow-wave,
Hills will suggest themselves. All such suggestions
Are yours to take or leave, but hear this warning:
Let them not be too velvet green, the fields
Which the deft needle of your eye appoints,
Nor the old farm past which you make your way
Too shady-linteled, too instinct with home.
It is precisely from Potemkin barns
With their fresh-painted hex signs on the gables,
Their sparkling gloom within, their stanchion-rattle
And sweet breath of silage, that there comes
The trotting cat whose head is but a skull.
Try to remember this: what you project
Is what you will perceive; what you perceive
With any passion, be it love or terror,
May take on whims and powers of its own.

Therefore a numb and grudging circumspection
Will serve you best, unless you overdo it,
Watching your step too narrowly, refusing
To specify a world, shrinking your purview
To a tight vision of your inching shoes –
Which may, as soon you come to think, be crossing
An unseen gorge upon a rotten trestle.
What you must manage is to bring to mind
A landscape not worth looking at, some bleak
Champaign at dead November's end, its grass
As dry as lichen, and its lichens grey,
Such glumly simple country that a glance
Of flat indifference from time to time
Will stabilize it. Lifeless thus, and leafless,
The view should set at rest all thoughts of ambush.
Nevertheless, permit no roadside thickets
Which, as you pass, might shake with worse than wind;
Revoke all trees and other cover; blast
The upstart boulder which a flicking shape
Has stepped behind; above all, put a stop
To the known stranger up ahead, whose face
Half turns to mark you with a creased expression.
Here let me interject that steady trudging
Can make you drowsy, so that without transition,
As when an old film jumps in the projector,

You will be wading a dun hallway, rounding
A newel post, and starting up the stairs.
Should that occur, adjust to circumstances
And carry on, taking these few precautions:
Detach some portion of your thought to guard
The outside of the building; as you wind
From room to room, leave nothing at your back,
But slough all memories at every threshold;
Nor must you dream of opening any door
Until you have foreseen what lies beyond it.
Regardless of its seeming size, or what
May first impress you as its style or function,
The abrupt structure which involves you now
Will improvise like vapor. Groping down
The gritty cellar steps and past the fuse-box,
Brushing through sheeted lawn-chairs, you emerge
In some cathedral's pillared crypt, and thence,
Your brow alight with carbide, pick your way
To the main shaft through drifts and rubbly tunnels.
Promptly the hoist, ascending toward the pit-head,
Rolls downward past your gaze a dinted rock-face
Peppered with hacks and drill-holes, which acquire
Insensibly the look of hieroglyphics.
Whether to surface now within the vast
Stone tent where Cheops lay secure, or take
The proffered shed of corrugated iron
Which gives at once upon a vacant barracks,

Is up to you. Need I, at this point, tell you
What to avoid? Avoid the pleasant room
Where someone, smiling to herself, has placed
A bowl of yellow freesias. Do not let
The thought of her in yellow, lithe and sleek
As lemonwood, mislead you where the curtains,
Romping like spinnakers which taste the wind,
Bellying out and lifting till the sill
Has shipped a drench of sunlight, then subsiding,
Both warm and cool the love-bed. Your concern
Is not to be detained by dread, or by
Such dear acceptances as would entail it,
But to pursue an ever-dimming course
Of pure transition, treading as in water
Past crumbling tufa, down cloacal halls
Of boarded-up hotels, through attics full
Of glassy taxidermy, moping on
Like a drugged fire-inspector. What you hope for
Is that at some point of the pointless journey,
Indoors or out, and when you least expect it,
Right in the middle of your stride, like that,
So neatly that you never feel a thing,
The kind assassin Sleep will draw a bead
And blow your brains out.

               What, are you still awake?
Then you must risk another tack and footing.
Forget what I have said. Open your eyes

To the good blackness not of your room alone
But of the sky you trust is over it,
Whose stars, though foundering in the time to come,
Bequeath us constantly a jetsam beauty.
Now with your knuckles rub your eyelids, seeing
The phosphenes caper like St. Elmo's fire,
And let your head heel over on the pillow
Like a flung skiff on wild Gennesaret.
Let all things storm your thought with the moiled
        flocking
Of startled rookeries, or flak in air,
Or blossom-fall, and out of that come striding
In the strong dream by which you have been chosen.
Are you upon the roads again? If so,
Be led past honeyed meadows which might tempt
A wolf to graze, and groves which are not you
But answer to your suppler self, that nature
Able to bear the thrush's quirky glee
In stands of chuted light, yet praise as well,
All leaves aside, the barren bark of winter.
When, as you may, you find yourself approaching
A crossroads and its laden gallows tree,
Do not with hooded eyes allow the shadow
Of a man moored in air to bruise your forehead,
But lift your gaze and stare your brother down,
Though the swart crows have pecked his sockets
        hollow.

As for what turn your travels then will take,
I cannot guess. Long errantry perhaps
Will arm you to be gentle, or the claws
Of nightmare flap you pathless God knows where,
As the crow flies, to meet your dearest horror.
Still, if you are in luck, you may be granted,
As, inland, one can sometimes smell the sea,
A moment's perfect carelessness, in which
To stumble a few steps and sink to sleep
In the same clearing where, in the old story,
A holy man discovered Vishnu sleeping,
Wrapped in his maya, dreaming by a pool
On whose calm face all images whatever
Lay clear, unfathomed, taken as they came.

THE TWIN OF SLEEP

Death is the twin of Sleep, they say:
    For I shall rise renewed,
Free from the cramps of yesterday,
    Clear-eyed and supple-thewed.

But though this bland analogy
    Helps other folk to face
Decrepitude, senility,
    Madness, disease, disgrace,

I do not like Death's greedy looks:
    Give me his twin instead –
Sleep never auctions off my books,
    My boots, my shirts, my bed.

THE SLEEP THAT COMES OVER ME

The sleep that comes over me,
The mental sleep that physically hits me,
The universal sleep that personally overcomes me –
To others
Such a sleep must seem a sleep to fall asleep in,
The sleep of someone wanting to go to sleep,
The very sleep that is sleep.

But it's more, it goes deeper, higher than that:
It's the sleep encompassing every disappointment.
It's the sleep that synthesizes all despair,
It's the sleep of feeling there's a world within me
Without my having said yes or no to it.

Yet the sleep that comes over me
Is just like ordinary sleep.
Being tired at least softens you,
Being run-down at least quiets you,
Giving up at least puts an end to trying,
And the end at least is giving up having to hope.

There's the sound of a window opening.
Indifferent, I turn my head to the left,
Looking over the shoulder that felt it,
And see through the half-opened window

The girl on the third floor across the street
Leaning out, her blue eyes searching for someone.
Who?
My indifference asks.
And all this is sleep.

My God, so much sleep!...

LINES

How lovely is the heaven of this night,
How deadly still its earth. The forest brute
Has crept into his cave, and laid himself
Where sleep has made him harmless like the lamb:
The horrid snake, his venom now forgot,
Is still and innocent as the honied flower
Under his head: – and man, in whom are met
Leopard and snake, – and all the gentleness
And beauty of the young lamb and the bud,
Has let his ghost out, put his thoughts aside
And lent his senses unto death himself;
Whereby the King and beggar all lie down
On straw or purple-tissue, are but bones
And air, and blood, equal to one another
And to the unborn and buried: so we go
Placing ourselves among the unconceived
And the old ghosts, wantonly, smilingly,
For sleep is fair and warm.

SLEEPERS

THE SEA OF SLEEP

Some float gently ashore. They lie
with their shoulders on the sand
till the sea ebbs.

Others splash violently through the shallows
and collapse panting
at high water mark.

I, king dolphin of the sea of sleep,
leap ashore – rising in air as dolphin,
landing as man.

I visit the huts of the natives
and eat their strange foods, and
keep looking out to sea

where this lumpish man was frolicsome
in a school of dreams – black hoops, submerging, then
slithering up into the light and scattering it.

SONG

See, how like twilight slumber falls
T' obscure the glory of those balls,
      And, as she sleeps,
      See how light creeps
Thorough the chinks, and beautifies
The rayie fringe of her fair eyes.

Observe Love's feuds, how fast they fly,
To every heart, from her clos'd eye,
      What then will she,
      When waking, be?
A glowing light for all t' admire,
Such as would set the world on fire.

Then seal her eyelids, gentle Sleep,
Whiles cares of her mine open keep;
      Lock up, I say
      Those doors of day,
Which with the morn for lustre strive,
That I may look on her, and live.

A FRIEND STAYS THE NIGHT

Rinsing sorrows of a thousand forevers
away, we linger out a hundred jars of wine,

the clear night's clarity filling small talk,
a lucid moon keeping us awake. And after

we're drunk, we sleep in empty mountains,
all heaven our blanket, earth our pillow.

ON PAINTING

I attend to my work and I love it.
But today the languor of composition disheartens me.
The day has affected me. Its face
is deepening dark. It continues to blow and rain.
I would sooner see than speak.
In this painting now, I am looking at
a beautiful lad who is stretched out
near the fountain, probably worn out from running.
What a beautiful child; what a divine noon
has now overtaken him to lull him to sleep. –
I sit and look so for a long time.
And again it is in art that I rest from its toil.

A CHILD'S SLEEP

As light on a lake's face moving
   Between a cloud and a cloud
Till night reclaim it, reproving
   The heart that exults too loud,

The heart that watching rejoices
   When soft it swims into sight
Applauded of all the voices
   And stars of the windy night,

So brief and unsure, but sweeter
   Than ever a moondawn smiled,
Moves, measured of no tune's metre,
   The song in the soul of a child;

The song that the sweet soul singing
   Half listens, and hardly hears,
Though sweeter than joy-bells ringing
   And brighter than joy's own tears;

The song that remembrance of pleasure
   Begins, and forgetfulness ends
With a soft swift change in the measure
   That rings in remembrance of friends.

As the moon on the lake's face flashes,
    So haply may gleam at whiles
A dream through the dear deep lashes
    Whereunder a child's eye smiles,

And the least of us all that love him
    May take for a moment part
With angels around and above him,
    And I find place in his heart.

THE SLEEPER

What a strange lump of laziness here lies,
That from the light of day bolts up his eyes!
Thou look'st, when God created thee, as if
He had forgot t' impart His breath of life.
That th' art with seven sleepy Fiends possest,
A man would judge, or that bewitcht at least.
It is a curse upon thee, without doubt,
And Heav'n for sin has put thy candles out.

   I could excuse thee, if this sloth could be
Bred by the venom of infirmity;
But 'tis in Nature's force impossible,
Her whole corruption makes not such a spell,
Though thou an abstract had'st ingrost of all
Ills, and diseases apoplectical.

CHARLES COTTON (1630–87)   73

SLEEPING ON HER COUCH

Thus lovely, *Sleep* did *first* appear,
    E're yet it was with *Death* ally'd;
When the first *fair one*, like *her* here,
    Lay down, and for a little *dy'd.*

E're *happy Souls* knew how to *dye*,
    And trod the *rougher Paths* to *Bliss,*
Transported in an *Extasie*,
    They *breath'd out* such *smooth waies*, as this.

Her *Hand* bears gently up her *Head*,
    And like a *Pillow*, rais'd does keep;
But *softer* than her *Couch*, is spread,
    Though that be *softer*, than her *Sleep.*

Alas! that death-like *Sleep*, or *Night*,
    Should power have to close those *Eyes;*
Which once vy'd with the *fairest Light*,
    Or what *gay Colours*, thence did rise.

Ah! that lost *Beams*, thus long have shin'd,
    To them, with *Darkness* over-spread,
Unseen, as *Day breaks*, to the *Blind*,
    Or the *Sun rises*, to the *Dead.*

That *Sun*, in all his *Eastern Pride*,
    Did never see a *Shape* so rare,
Nor *Night*, within its *black Arms* hide
    A *silent Beauty*, half so *fair.*

THE SLEEPER

The Lovely, sleeping, lay in bed,
    Her limbs, from quiet foot to chin,
Still as the dust of one that's dead
    Whose spirit waits the entering-in.

Yet her young cheek with life's faint dye
    Was mantled o'er; her gentle breast
Like sea at peace with starry sky,
    Moved with a heart at rest.

Fair country of a thousand springs,
    Calm hill and vale! Those hidden eyes
And tongue that daylong talks and sings,
    Wait only for the sun to rise.

Let but a bird call in that ear,
    Let beam of day that window wan,
This hidden one will, wakening, hear,
    And deathlike slumber-swoon be gone:

Her ardent eyes once more will shine,
    She will uplift her hair-crowned head;
At lip, miraculous, life's wine,
    At hand, its wondrous bread.

WALTER DE LA MARE (1873–1956)   75

LOVE LIES SLEEPING

Earliest morning, switching all the tracks
that cross the sky from cinder star to star,
    coupling the ends of streets
    to trains of light,

now draw us into daylight in our beds;
and clear away what presses on the brain:
    put out the neon shapes
    that float and swell and glare

down the gray avenue between the eyes
in pinks and yellows, letters and twitching signs.
    Hang-over moons, wane, wane!
    From the window I see

an immense city, carefully revealed,
made delicate by over-workmanship,
    detail upon detail,
    cornice upon façade,

reaching so languidly up into
a weak white sky, it seems to waver there.
    (Where it has slowly grown
    in skies of water-glass

from fused beads of iron and copper crystals,
the little chemical 'garden' in a jar
    trembles and stands again,
    pale blue, blue-green, and brick.)

The sparrows hurriedly begin their play.
Then, in the West, 'Boom!' and a cloud of smoke.
    'Boom!' and the exploding ball
    of blossom blooms again.

(And all the employees who work in plants
where such a sound says 'Danger,' or once said 'Death,'
    turn in their sleep and feel
    the short hairs bristling

on backs of necks.) The cloud of smoke moves off.
A shirt is taken off a threadlike clothes-line.
    Along the street below
    the water-wagon comes

throwing its hissing, snowy fan across
peelings and newspapers. The water dries
    light-dry, dark-wet, the pattern
    of the cool watermelon.

I hear the day-springs of the morning strike
from stony walls and halls and iron beds,
    scattered or grouped cascades,
    alarms for the expected:

queer cupids of all persons getting up,
whose evening meal they will prepare all day,
    you will dine well
    on his heart, on his, and his,

so send them about your business affectionately,
dragging in the streets their unique loves.
    Scourge them with roses only,
    be light as helium,

for always to one, or several, morning comes,
whose head has fallen over the edge of his bed,
    whose face is turned
    so that the image of

the city grows down into his open eyes
inverted and distorted. No. I mean
    distorted and revealed,
    if he sees it at all.

LA BELLE AU BOIS DORMANT

She lies, her head beneath her knees,
In their old trunk; and no one comes –
No porter, even, with a check
Or forceps for her hard delivery.
The trains pant outside; and she coils breathlessly
Inside his wish and is not waked.

She is sleeping but, alas! not beautiful.
Travelers doze around; are borne away;
And the thorns clamber up her stony veins.
She is irreparable; and yet a state
Asks for her absently, and citizens
Drown for an instant in her papery eyes.

Yet where is the hunter black enough to storm
Her opening limbs, or shudder like a fish
Into the severed maelstrom of her skull?
The blood fondles her outrageous mouth;
The lives flourish in her life, to alienate
Their provinces from her outranging smile.

What wish, what keen pain has enchanted her
To this cold period, the end of pain,
Wishes, enchantment: this suspending sleep?
She waits here to be waked – as he has waited
For her to wake, for her to wake –
Her lips set in their slack conclusive smile.

RANDALL JARRELL (1914–65)   79

SLEEPING

The princess was baptised inside a shell,
Nude, adult, rich and handsome, but a bitch.
Small wonder she refused to ask that witch
Who scuttled lecherous tars, dried up a well
That poisoned villagers, silenced the bell
Of the smug church and moved fat squashy cows
Whole fields away to give a poor man's house
Milk for a week! really, one just can't tell
This story after all the palace lies.
There was no curse. The princess sighed, and rust
Crumbled the pantry lock. The king yawned. Flies
Settled on footmen turned to snoring dust.
Churls grinned. Till through them, too, there flowed
    the deep
And uncontrollable desire to sleep.

ON A BIRD SINGING IN ITS SLEEP

A bird half wakened in the lunar noon
Sang half way through its little inborn tune.
Partly because it sang but once all night
And that from no especial bush's height;
Partly because it sang ventriloquist
And had the inspiration to desist
Almost before the prick of hostile ears,
It ventured less in peril than appears.
It could not have come down to us so far
Through the interstices of things ajar
On the long bead chain of repeated birth
To be a bird while we are men on earth
If singing out of sleep and dream that way
Had made it much more easily a prey.

ROBERT FROST (1874–1963)

FOOTSTEPS

On an ebony bed, ornamented
with coral eagles, sound asleep, lies
Nero – unconscious, quiet and blissful,
flourishing in the vigour of the flesh
and in the splendid strength of youth.

But in the alabaster hall enclosing
the ancient shrine of the Ahenobarbi
how restive are his Lares.
The small household gods tremble
and they try to hide their insignificant bodies.
For they heard a sinister clamour,
a deathly clamour ascending the stairs;
iron footsteps rattling the stairs.
And now in a faint the miserable Lares
bury themselves in the rear of the shrine;
one tumbles and stumbles over the other,
one little god falls over the other
for they understand what sort of clamour this is,
by now they already know the Furies' footsteps.

TRANSLATED BY RAE DALVEN

THE SLEEPOUT

Childhood sleeps in a verandah room
in an iron bed close to the wall
where the winter over the railing
swelled the blind on its timber boom

and splinters picked lint off warm linen
and the stars were out over the hill;
then one wall of the room was forest
and all things in there were to come.

Breathings climbed up on the verandah
when dark cattle rubbed at a corner
and sometimes dim towering rain stood
for forest, and the dry cave hunched woollen.

Inside the forest was lamplit
along tracks to a starry creek bed
and beyond lay the never-fenced country,
its full billabongs all surrounded

by animals and birds, in loud crustings,
and something kept leaping up amongst them.
And out there, to kindle whenever
dark found it, hung the daylight moon.

LES MURRAY (1938–   )   83

THE SLEEPER

As Ann came in one summer's day,
    She felt that she must creep,
So silent was the clear cool house,
    It seemed a house of sleep.
And sure, when she pushed-open the door,
    Rapt in the stillness there,
Her mother sat, with stooping head,
    Asleep upon a chair;
Fast – fast asleep; her two hands laid
    Loose-folded on her knee,
So that her small unconscious face
    Looked half unreal to be:
So calmly lit with sleep's pale light
    Each feature was; so fair
Her forehead – every trouble was
    Smoothed out beneath her hair.
But though her mind in dream now moved,
    Still seemed her gaze to rest –
From out beneath her fast-sealed lids,
    Above her moving breast –
On Ann; as quite, quite still she stood;
    Yet slumber lay so deep
Even her hands upon her lap
    Seemed saturate with sleep.

And as Ann peeped, a cloudlike dread
   Stole over her, and then,
On stealthy, mouselike feet she trod,
   And tiptoed out again.

Walter de la Mare (1873–1956)

ON A SLEEPING FRIEND

Lady, when your lovely head
Droops to sink among the Dead,
And the quiet places keep
You that so divinely sleep;
Then the dead shall blessèd be
With a new solemnity,
For such Beauty, so descending,
Pledges them that Death is ending.
Sleep your fill – but when you wake
Dawn shall over Lethe break.

Hilaire Belloc (1870–1953)

OF THE LADY WHO CAN SLEEP WHEN
SHE PLEASES

No wonder sleep from carefull lovers flies
To bathe himself in *Sacharissa's* eyes,
As fair Astrea once from earth to heaven
By strife and loud impiety was driven:
So with our plaints offended, and our tears,
Wife *Somnus* to that Paradise repairs,
Waits on her will, and wretches does forsake
To court the Nimph for whom those wretches wake:
More proud then *Phœbus* of his throne of gold
Is the soft god those softer limbs to hold.
Nor would exchange with *Jove* to hide the skies
In darkning clouds the power to close her eyes:
Eyes which so far all other lights controul,
They warm our mortall parts, but these our soul:
Let her free spirit whose unconquer'd breast
Holds such deep quiet and untroubled rest:
Know that though *Venus* and her son should spare
Her Rebell heart, and never teach her care:
Yet Hymen may inforce her vigils keep,
And for anothers joy suspend her sleep.

ASLEEP

Under his helmet, up against his pack,
After the many days of work and waking,
Sleep took him by the brow and laid him back.
And in the happy no-time of his sleeping,
Death took him by the heart. There was a quaking
Of the aborted life within him leaping ...
Then chest and sleepy arms once more fell slack.
And soon the slow, stray blood came creeping
From the intrusive lead, like ants on track.

Whether his deeper sleep lie shaded by the shaking
Of great wings, and the thoughts that hung the stars,
High pillowed on calm pillows of God's making
Above these clouds, these rains, these sleets of lead,
And these winds' scimitars;
– Or whether yet his thin and sodden head
Confuses more and more with the low mould,
His hair being one with the grey grass
And finished fields of autumns that are old ...
Who knows? Who hopes? Who troubles? Let it pass!
He sleeps. He sleeps less tremulous, less cold
Than we who must awake, and waking, say Alas!

WILFRED OWEN (1893–1918)

SLEEP AT SEA

Sound the deep waters: –
    Who shall sound that deep? –
Too short the plummet,
    And the watchmen sleep.
Some dream of effort
    Up a toilsome steep;
Some dream of pasture grounds
    For harmless sheep.

White shapes flit to and fro
    From mast to mast;
They feel the distant tempest
    That nears them fast:
Great rocks are straight ahead,
    Great shoals not past;
They shout to one another
    Upon the blast.

O, soft the streams drop music
    Between the hills,
And musical the birds' nests
    Beside those rills;
The nests are types of home
    Love-hidden from ills,
The nests are types of spirits
    Love-music fills.

So dream the sleepers,
    Each man in his place;
The lightning shows the smile
    Upon each face:
The ship is driving, driving,
    It drives apace:
And sleepers smile, and spirits
    Bewail their case.

The lightning glares and reddens
    Across the skies;
It seems but sunset
    To those sleeping eyes.
When did the sun go down
    On such a wise?
From such a sunset
    When shall day arise?

'Wake,' call the spirits:
    But to heedless ears;
They have forgotten sorrows
    And hopes and fears;
They have forgotten perils
    And smiles and tears;
Their dream has held them long
    Long years and years.

'Wake,' call the spirits again:
    But it would take
A louder summons
    To bid them awake.
Some dream of pleasure
    For another's sake;
Some dream, forgetful
    Of a lifelong ache.

One by one slowly,
    Ah, how sad and slow!
Wailing and praying
    The spirits rise and go:
Clear stainless spirits
    White, white as snow;
Pale spirits, wailing
    For an overthrow.

One by one flitting,
    Like a mournful bird
Whose song is tired at last
    For not mate heard.
The loving voice is silent,
    The useless word;
One by one flitting,
    Sick with hope deferred.

Driving and driving,
    The ship drives amain:
While swift from mast to mast
    Shapes flit again,
Flit silent as the silence
    Where men lie slain;
Their shadow cast upon the sails
    Is like a stain.

No voice to call the sleepers,
    No hand to raise:
They sleep to death in dreaming
    Of length of days.
Vanity of vanities,
    The Preacher says:
Vanity is the end
    Of all their ways.

CHRISTINA ROSSETTI (1830–94)

NUPTIAL SLEEP

NUPTIAL SLEEP

At length their long kiss severed, with sweet smart:
    And as the last slow sudden drops are shed
    From sparking eaves when all the storm has fled,
So singly flagged the pulses of each heart.
Their bosoms sundered, with the opening start
    Of married flowers to either side outspread
    From the knit stem; yet still their mouths, burnt red,
Fawned on each other where they lay apart.

Sleep sank them lower than the tide of dreams,
    And their dreams watched them sink, and slid away.
Slowly their souls swam up again, through gleams
    Of watered light and dull drowned waifs of day;
Till from some wonder of new woods and streams
    He woke, and wondered more: for there she lay.

FRIDAY NIGHT

On the brink of sleep, stretched in a wide bed,
    Rain pattering at the windows
And proud waves booming against granite rocks:
    Such was our night of glory.

Thursday had brought us dreams only of evil,
    As the muezzin warned us:
'Forget all nightmare once the dawn breaks,
    Prepare for holy Friday!'

Friday brings dreams only of inward love
    So overpassing passion
That no lips reach to kiss, nor hands to clasp,
    Nor does foot press on foot.

We wait until the lamp has flickered out
    Leaving us in full darkness,
Each still observant of the other's lively
    Sighs of pure content.

Truth is prolonged until the grey dawn:
    Her face floating above me,
Her black hair falling cloudlike to her breasts,
    Her lovely eyes half-open.

THE SHRIKE

When night comes black
Such royal dreams beckon this man
As lift him apart
From his earth-wife's side
To wing, sleep-feathered,
The singular air,
While she, envious bride,
Cannot follow after, but lies
With her blank brown eyes starved wide,
Twisting curses in the tangled sheet
With taloned fingers,
Shaking in her skull's cage
The stuffed shape of her flown mate
Escaped among moon-plumaged strangers;
So hungered, she must wait in rage
Until bird-racketing dawn
When her shrike-face
Leans to peck open those locked lids, to eat
Crowns, palace, all
That nightlong stole her male,
And with red beak
Spike and suck out
Last blood-drop of that truant heart.

SLEEP WRAPPED YOU

Sleep wrapped you in green leaves like a tree
you breathed like a tree in the quiet light
in the limpid spring I looked at your face:
eyelids closed, eyelashes brushing the water.
In the soft grass my fingers found your fingers
I held your pulse a moment
and felt elsewhere your heart's pain.

Under the plane tree, near the water, among laurel
sleep moved you and scattered you
around me, near me, without my being able to touch
    the whole of you —
one as you were with your silence;
seeing your shadow grow and diminish,
lose itself in the other shadows, in the other
world that let you go yet held you back.

The life that they gave us to live, we lived.
Pity those who wait with such patience
lost in the black laurel under the heavy plane trees
and those, alone, who speak to cisterns and wells
and drown in the voice's circles.
Pity the companion who shared our privation and
    our sweat
and plunged into the sun like a crow beyond the ruins,
without hope of enjoying our reward.

Give us, outside sleep, serenity.

98   GEORGE SEFERIS (1900–71)

    TRANSLATED BY EDMUND KEELEY AND
    PHILIP SHERRARD

LOVE AND SLEEP

Lying asleep between the strokes of night
   I saw my love lean over my sad bed,
   Pale as the duskiest lily's leaf or head,
Smooth-skinned and dark, with bare throat made to
     bite,
Too wan for blushing and too warm for white,
   But perfect-coloured without white or red.
   And her lips opened amorously, and said –
I wist not what, saving one word – Delight.
And all her face was honey to my mouth,
   And all her body pasture to mine eyes;
     The long lithe arms and hotter hands than fire,
The quivering flanks, hair smelling of the south,
   The bright light feet, the splendid supple thighs
     And glittering eyelids of my soul's desire.

ALGERNON CHARLES SWINBURNE (1837–1909)   99

TOUCH

You are already
asleep. I lower
myself in next to
you, my skin slightly
numb with the restraint
of habits, the patina of
self, the black frost
of outsideness, so that even
unclothed it is
a resilient chilly
hardness, a superficially
malleable, dead
rubbery texture.

You are a mound
of bedclothes, where the cat
in sleep braces
its paws against your
calf through the blankets,
and kneads each paw in turn.

Meanwhile and slowly
I feel a is it
my own warmth surfacing or
the ferment of your whole
body that in darkness beneath
the cover is stealing

bit by bit to break
down that chill.

        You turn and
hold me tightly, do
you know who
I am or am I
your mother or
the nearest human being to
hold on to in a
dreamed pogrom.

What I, now loosened,
sink into is an old
big place, it is
there already, for
you are already
there, and the cat
got there before you, yet
it is hard to locate.
What is more, the place is
not found but seeps
from our touch in
continuous creation, dark
enclosing cocoon round
ourselves alone, dark
wide realm where we
walk with everyone.

THOM GUNN (1929–   )

THE DREAM

I met her as a blossom on a stem
Before she ever breathed, and in that dream
The mind remembers from a deeper sleep:
Eye learned from eye, cold lip from sensual lip.
My dream divided on a point of fire;
Light hardened on the water where we were;
A bird sang low; the moonlight sifted in;
The water rippled, and she rippled on.

She came toward me in the flowing air,
A shape of change, encircled by its fire.
I watched her there, between me and the moon;
The bushes and the stones danced on and on;
I touched her shadow when the light delayed;
I turned my face away, and yet she stayed.
A bird sang from the center of a tree;
She loved the wind because the wind loved me.

Love is not love until love's vulnerable.
She slowed to sigh, in that long interval.
A small bird flew in circles where we stood;
The deer came down, out of the dappled wood.
All who remember, doubt. Who calls that strange?
I tossed a stone, and listened to its plunge.
She knew the grammar of least motion, she
Lent me one virtue, and I live thereby.

She held her body steady in the wind;
Our shadows met, and slowly swung around;
She turned the field into a glittering sea;
I played in flame and water like a boy
And I swayed out beyond the white seafoam;
Like a wet log, I sang within a flame.
In that last while, eternity's confine,
I came to love, I came into my own.

THEODORE ROETHKE (1908–63)   103

SLEEPING WITH YOU

One creature, not the mollusk
clamped around an orgasm, but
more loosely biune, we are linked
by tugs of the blanket and dreams whose disquiet
unsettles night's oily depths, creating
those eddies of semi-wakefulness wherein
we acknowledge the other is there
as an arm is there, or an ancestor,
or any fact admitted yet not known.

What body is warm beside mine,
what corpse has been slain
on this soft battlefield where we wounded
lift our heads to cry for water
and to ask what forces prevailed?
It is you, not dead, but entrusted
at my side to the flight the chemical mind
must take or be crazed, leaving the body
behind like matériel in a trench.

The moon throws back sunlight into the woods,
but whiter, cleansed by its bounce
amid the cold stars, and the owls
fly their unthinkable paths to pluck
the velvet mole from her tunnel of leaves.

Dreaming rotates us, but fear
leads us to cling each to each as a spar
is clung to by the shipwrecked
till dawn brings sky-fire and rescue.

Your breathing, relaxed to its center,
scrapes like a stone on rough fiber,
over and over. Your skin, steeped
in its forgetting, sweats,
and flurries of footwork bring you near
the surface; but then your rapt lungs slip
with a sigh back into the healing,
that unpoliced swirling of spirit
whose sharing is a synonym for love.

JOHN UPDIKE (1932–   )   105

THE SLEEPERS

No map traces the street
Where those two sleepers are.
We have lost track of it.
They lie as if under water
In a blue, unchanging light,
The French window ajar

Curtained with yellow lace.
Through the narrow crack
Odors of wet earth rise.
The snail leaves a silver track;
Dark thickets hedge the house.
We take a backward look.

Among petals pale as death
And leaves steadfast in shape
They sleep on, mouth to mouth.
A white mist is going up.
The small green nostrils breathe,
And they turn in their sleep.

Ousted from that warm bed
We are a dream they dream.
Their eyelids keep the shade.
No harm can come to them.
We cast our skins and slide
Into another time.

THE HUG

It was your birthday, we had drunk and dined
    Half of the night with our old friend
        Who'd showed us in the end
    To a bed I reached in one drunk stride.
        Already I lay snug,
And drowsy with the wine dozed on one side.

I dozed, I slept. My sleep broke on a hug,
        Suddenly, from behind,
In which the full lengths of our bodies pressed:
        Your instep to my heel,
    My shoulder-blades against your chest.
    It was not sex, but I could feel
    The whole strength of your body set,
        Or braced, to mine,
        And locking me to you
    As if we were still twenty-two
    When our grand passion had not yet
        Become familial.
    My quick sleep had deleted all
    Of intervening time and place.
        I only knew
The stay of your secure firm dry embrace.

THOM GUNN (1929–   )

TEARS IN SLEEP

All night the cocks crew, under a moon like day,
And I, in the cage of sleep, on a stranger's breast,
Shed tears, like a task not to be put away –
In the false light, false grief in my happy bed,
A labor of tears, set against joy's undoing.
I would not wake at your word, I had tears to say.
I clung to the bars of the dream and they were said,
And pain's derisive hand had given me rest
From the night giving off flames, and the dark
     renewing.

THE STILLY NIGHT: A SOPORIFIC
REFLECTION

He unwinds himself from the bedclothes each morn and
    piteously proclaims that he didn't sleep a wink, and
    she gives him a glance savage and murderous

And replies that it was she who didn't close an eye until
    cockcrow because of his swinish slumber as evi-
    denced by his snores continuous and stertorous,

And his indignation is unconcealed,

He says she must have dreamed that one up during
    her night-long sweet repose, which he was fully
    conscious of because for eight solid hours he had
    listened to her breathing not quite so gentle as a
    zephyr on a flowery field.

The fact is that she did awaken twice for brief intervals
    and he was indeed asleep and snoring, and he did
    awaken similarly and she was indeed unconscious
    and breathing miscellaneously,

But they were never both awake simultaneously.

Oh, sleep it is a blessed thing, but not to those wakeful
    ones who watch their mates luxuriating in it when
    they feel that their own is sorely in arrears.

I am certain that the first words of the Sleeping Beauty
    to her prince were, 'You *would* have to kiss me just
    when I had dropped off after tossing and turning
    for a hundred years.'

OGDEN NASH (1902–71)   109

THE NEAREST
DREAM

THE NEAREST DREAM

The nearest Dream recedes – unrealized –
The Heaven we chase,
Like the June Bee – before the School Boy,
Invites the Race –
Stoops – to an easy Clover –
Dips – evades – teases – deploys –
Then – to the Royal Clouds
Lifts his light Pinnace –
Heedless of the Boy –
Staring – bewildered – at the mocking sky –
Homesick for steadfast Honey –
Ah, the Bee flies not
That brews that rare variety!

EMILY DICKINSON (1830–86)   113

DREAMS

'Tis strange! I saw the Skies;
I saw the Hills before mine Eys;
The Sparrow fly;
The Lands that did about me ly;
The reall Sun, *that* hev'nly Ey!
Can closed Eys ev'n in the darkest Night
See throu their Lids, and be inform'd with Sight?

The Peeple were to me
As tru as those by day I see;
As tru the Air,
The Earth as sweet, as fresh, as fair
As that which did by day repair
Unto my waking Sense! Can all the Sky,
Can all the World, within my Brain-pan ly?

What sacred Secret's this,
Which seems to intimat my Bliss?
What is there in
The narrow Confines of my Skin,
That is alive and feels within
When I am dead? Can Magnitude possess
An activ Memory, yet not be less?

May all that I can see
Awake, by Night within me be?
　　　My Childhood knew
No Difference, but all was Tru,
As Reall all as what I view;
The World its Self was there. 'Twas wondrous strange,
That Hev'n and Earth should so their place exchange.

Till *that* which vulgar Sense
Doth falsly call Experience,
　　　Distinguisht things:
The Ribbans, and the gaudy Wings
Of Birds, the Virtues, and the Sins,
That represented were in Dreams by night
As really my Senses did delight,

Or griev, as those I saw
By day: Things terrible did aw
　　　My Soul with Fear;
The Apparitions seem'd as near
As Things could be, and Things they were:
Yet were they all by Fancy in me wrought,
And all their Being founded in a Thought.

O what a Thing is Thought!
Which seems a Dream; yea, seemeth Nought,
　　　Yet doth the Mind

Affect as much as what we find
　　Most near and tru! Sure Men are blind,
And can't the forcible Reality
Of things that Secret are within them see.

　　　Thought! Surely *Thoughts* are tru;
　　They pleas as much as *Things* can do:
　　　　　Nay Things are dead,
　　And in themselvs are severèd
　　From Souls; nor can they fill the Head
Without our Thoughts. Thoughts are the Reall things
From whence all Joy, from whence all Sorrow springs.

From THE RAPE OF THE LOCK

Sol thro' white Curtains shot a tim'rous Ray,
And op'd those Eyes that must eclipse the Day;
Now Lapdogs give themselves the rowzing Shake,
And sleepless Lovers, just at Twelve, awake:
Thrice rung the Bell, the Slipper knock'd the Ground,
And the press'd Watch return'd a silver Sound.
Belinda still her downy Pillow prest,
Her Guardian *Sylph* prolong'd the balmy Rest.
'Twas he had summon'd to her silent Bed
The Morning-Dream that hover'd o'er her Head.
A Youth more glitt'ring than a *Birth-night Beau,*
(That ev'n in Slumber caus'd her Cheek to glow)
Seem'd to her Ear his winning Lips to lay,
And thus in Whispers said, or seem'd to say.

    Fairest of Mortals, thou distinguish'd Care
Of thousand bright Inhabitants of Air!
If e'er one Vision touch'd thy infant Thought,
Of all the Nurse and all the Priest have taught,
Of airy Elves by Moonlight Shadows seen,
The silver Token, and the circled Green,
Or Virgins visited by Angel-Pow'rs,
With Golden Crowns and Wreaths of heavn'ly Flow'rs,
Hear and believe! thy own Importance know,
Nor bound thy narrow Views to Things below.
Some secret Truths from Learned Pride conceal'd,

To Maids alone and Children are reveal'd:
What tho' no Credit doubting Wits may give?
The Fair and Innocent shall still believe.
Know then, unnumber'd Spirits round thee fly,
The light *Militia* of the lower Sky;
These, tho' unseen, are ever on the Wing,
Hang o'er the *Box*, and hover round the *Ring*.
Think what an Equipage thou hast in Air,
And view with scorn *Two Pages* and a *Chair*.
As now your own, our Beings were of old,
And once inclos'd in Woman's beauteous Mold;
Thence, by a soft Transition, we repair
From earthly Vehicles to these of Air.
Think not, when Woman's transient Breath is fled,
That all her Vanities at once are dead:
Succeeding Vanities she still regards,
And tho' she plays no more, o'erlooks the Cards.
Her Joy in gilded Chariots, when alive,
And Love of *Ombre*, after Death survive.
For when the Fair in all their Pride expire,
To their first Elements their Souls retire:
The Sprights of fiery Termagants in Flame
Mount up, and take a *Salamander*'s Name.
Soft yielding Minds to Water glide away,
And sip with *Nymphs*, their Elemental Tea.
The graver Prude sinks downward to a *Gnome*,
In search of Mischief still on Earth to roam.

The light Coquettes in *Sylphs* aloft repair,
And sport and flutter in the Fields of Air.

Know farther yet; Whoever fair and chaste
Rejects Mankind, is by some *Sylph* embrac'd:
For Spirits, freed from mortal Laws, with ease
Assume what Sexes and what Shapes they please.
What guards the Purity of melting Maids,
In Courtly Balls, and Midnight Masquerades,
Safe from the treach'rous Friend, the daring Spark,
The Glance by Day, the Whisper in the Dark;
When kind Occasion prompts their warm Desires,
When Musick softens, and when Dancing fires?
'Tis but their *Sylph*, the wise Celestials know,
Tho' *Honour* is the Word with Men below.

Some Nymphs there are, too conscious of their Face,
For Life predestin'd to the *Gnomes'* Embrace.
These swell their Prospects and exalt their Pride,
When Offers are disdain'd, and Love deny'd.
Then gay Ideas crowd the vacant Brain;
While Peers and Dukes, and all their sweeping Train,
And Garters, Stars and Coronets appear,
And in soft Sounds, *Your Grace* salutes their Ear.
'Tis these that early taint the Female Soul,
Instruct the Eyes of young *Coquettes* to roll,
Teach Infant-Cheeks a bidden Blush to know,
And little Hearts to flutter at a *Beau.*

Oft when the World imagine Women stray,

The *Sylphs* thro' mystick Mazes guide their Way,
Thro' all the giddy Circle they pursue,
And old Impertinence expel by new.
What tender Maid but must a Victim fall
To one Man's Treat, but for another's Ball?
When *Florio* speaks, what Virgin could withstand,
If gentle *Damon* did not squeeze her Hand?
With varying Vanities, from ev'ry Part,
They shift the moving Toyshop of their Heart;
Where Wigs with Wigs, with Sword-knots
Sword-knots strive,
Beaus banish Beaus, and Coaches Coaches drive.
This erring Mortals Levity may call,
Oh blind to Truth! the *Sylphs* contrive it all.

Of these am I, who thy Protection claim,
A watchful Sprite, and *Ariel* is my Name.
Late, as I rang'd the Crystal Wilds of Air,
In the clear Mirror of thy ruling *Star*
I saw, alas! some dread Event impend,
Ere to the Main this Morning Sun descend.
But Heav'n reveals not what, or how, or where:
Warn'd by thy *Sylph*, oh Pious Maid beware!
This to disclose is all thy Guardian can.
Beware of all, but most beware of Man!

He said; when *Shock*, who thought she slept too long,
Leapt up, and wak'd his Mistress with his Tongue.
'Twas then *Belinda*! if Report say true,

Thy Eyes first open'd on a *Billet-doux*;
Wounds, Charms, and *Ardors,* were no sooner read
But all the Vision vanish'd from thy Head.

A DREAM OF MOUNTAINEERING

Written when he was seventy

At night, in my dream, I stoutly climbed a mountain,
Going out alone with my staff of holly-wood.
A thousand crags, a hundred hundred valleys –
In my dream-journey none were unexplored
And all the while my feet never grew tired
And my step was as strong as in my young days.
Can it be that when the mind travels backward
The body also returns to its old state?
And can it be, as between body and soul,
That the body may languish, while the soul is still
    strong?
Soul and body – both are vanities;
Dreaming and waking – both alike unreal.
In the day my feet are palsied and tottering;
In the night my steps go striding over the hills.
As day and night are divided in equal parts –
Between the two, I *get* as much as I *lose*.

TRANSLATED BY ARTHUR WALEY

THE KIND GHOSTS

She sleeps on soft, last breaths; but no ghost looms
Out of the stillness of her palace wall,
Her wall of boys on boys and dooms on dooms.

She dreams of golden gardens and sweet glooms,
Not marvelling why her roses never fall
Nor what red mouths were torn to make their blooms.

The shades keep down which well might roam her hall.
Quiet their blood lies in her crimson rooms
And she is not afraid of their footfall.

They move not from her tapestries, their pall,
Nor pace her terraces, their hecatombs,
Lest aught she be disturbed, or grieved at all.

WILFRED OWEN (1893–1918)   123

DREAMS IN MIDDLE AGE

Sooner let nightmares whinny, if we cannot
Retrieve our dreams of dalliance. Gloom or green,
We have been drowned or blinded, we have seen
Our springtime lady in her ringtime arbour,
We have been turned to stone or flown through
      chanting trees,
We have been present at the Crucifixion.
Such make have been our dreams – but what are these?

The debris of the day before; the faces
Come stuttering back while we ourselves remain
Ourselves or less, who, totting up in vain
The nightlong figures of the daylong ledger,
Stick at a point. Our lives are bursting at the seams
With petty detail. Thus we live, if living
Means that, and thus we dream – if these are dreams.

No, sooner let the dark engulf us. Sooner
Let the black horses, spluttering fire, stampede
Through home and office, let the fierce hands feed
Our dying values to the undying furnace.
The watch will stop and mark the red cross on the door
And cry 'Bring out your dead!' at any and every
      moment,
Unless we can be ourselves – ourselves or more.

IN THE WOOD

The field was clouded with a lilac heat.
Through the wood rolled the darkness of cathedrals.
What in the world remained for them to kiss?
It was all theirs, like soft wax in their fingers.

This is the dream, – you do not sleep, but dream
you thirst for sleep, that there's a fellow dozing
and through his dream from underneath his eyelids
a pair of black suns break and burn his lashes.

Their beams flowed by. And iridescent beetles.
The glass of dragon-flies roamed over cheeks.
The wood was full of tiny scintillations,
as at the clockmaker's beneath his tweezers.

It seemed he slumbered to the figures' tick,
while high above his head in harshest amber
they place in ether strictly tested clocks
and regulate them to the change of heat.

They shift them round about and shake the needles
and scatter shadow, swing and bore a place
for the tall masts' gloom, that's climbed into the day's
fatigue and lies across the deep blue dial.

It seemed that ancient joys were flying over,
sunset of dreams once more embraced the wood.
But happy people do not watch the clocks;
it seems they only lie in pairs and sleep.

BORIS PASTERNAK (1890–1960)   125

TRANSLATED BY J. M. COHEN

DREAM

After coming on Jerome S. Shipman's comment concerning academic appointments for artists.

The committee – now a permanent body –
        formed to do but one thing,
discover positions for artists, was worried, then happy;
rejoiced to have magnetized Bach and his family
  'to Northwestern,' besides five harpsichords
        without which he would not leave home.
For his methodic unmetronomic melodic diversity
contrapuntally appointedly persistently
        irresistibly Fate-like Bach – find me words.

Expected to create for university
        occasions, inventions with wing,
was no trouble after master-classes (stiffer in Germany),

each week a cantata; chorales, fugues, concerti!
  Here, students craved a teacher and each student
    worked.
        Jubilation! Re-rejoicings! Felicity!
        Repeated fugue-like, all of it, to infinity.
  (Note too that over-worked Bach was not irked.)

Haydn, when he had heard of Bach's billowing sail,
begged Prince Esterházy to lend him to Yale.
Master-mode expert fugue-al forms since, prevail.

> Dazzling nonsense ... I imagine it? Ah! nach
> enough. J. Sebastian – born at Eisenach:
> its coat-of-arms in my dream: BACH PLAYS BACH!

THE MAD SCENE

Again last night I dreamed the dream called Laundry.
In it, the sheets and towels of a life we were going to
      share,
The milk-stiff bibs, the shroud, each rag to be ever
Trampled or soiled, bled on or groped for blindly,
Came swooning out of an enormous willow hamper
Onto moon-marbly boards. We had just met. I watched
From outer darkness. I had dressed myself in clothes
Of a new fiber that never stains or wrinkles, never
Wears thin. The opera house sparkled with tiers
And tiers of eyes, like mine enlarged by belladonna,
Trained inward. There I saw the cloud-clot, gust by
      gust,
Form, and the lightning bite, and the roan mane
      unloosen.
Fingers were running in panic over the flute's nine
      gates.
Why did I flinch? I loved you. And in the downpour
      laughed
To have us wrung white, gnarled together, one
Topmost mordent of wisteria,
As the lean tree burst into grief.

THE VISION

Sitting alone, as one forsook,
Close by a silver-shedding brook,
With hands held up to love, I wept;
And after sorrows spent I slept:
Then in a vision I did see
A glorious form appear to me:
A virgin's face she had; her dress
Was like a sprightly Spartaness.
A silver bow, with green silk strung,
Down from her comely shoulders hung:
And as she stood, the wanton air
Dangled the ringlets of her hair.
Her legs were such Diana shows
When, tucked up, she a-hunting goes;
With buskins shortened to descry
The happy dawning of her thigh:
Which when I saw, I made access
To kiss that tempting nakedness:
But she forbade me with a wand
Of myrtle she had in her hand:
And, chiding me, said: Hence, remove,
Herrick, thou art too coarse to love.

ROBERT HERRICK (1591–1674)   129

IN PROCESSION

Often, half-way to sleep,
Not yet sunken deep –
The sudden moment on me comes
From a mountain shagged and steep,
With terrible roll of dream drums,
Reverberations, cymbals, horns replying,
When with standards flying,
Horsemen in clouds behind,
The coloured pomps unwind
Carnival wagons
With their saints and their dragons
On the scroll of my teeming mind:
The Creation and Flood
With our Saviour's Blood
And fat Silenus' flagons,
And every rare beast
From the South and East,
Both greatest and least,
On and on,
In endless, variant procession.

THE ANNIHILATION OF NOTHING

Nothing remained: Nothing, the wanton name
That nightly I rehearsed till led away
To a dark sleep, or sleep that held one dream.

In this a huge contagious absence lay,
More space than space, over the cloud and slime,
Defined but by the encroachments of its sway.

Stripped to indifference at the turns of time,
Whose end I knew, I woke without desire,
And welcomed zero as a paradigm.

But now it breaks – images burst with fire
Into the quiet sphere where I have bided,
Showing the landscape holding yet entire:

The power that I envisaged, that presided
Ultimate in its abstract devastations,
Is merely change, the atoms it divided

Complete, in ignorance, new combinations.
Only an infinite finitude I see
In those peculiar lovely variations.

It is despair that nothing cannot be
Flares in the mind and leaves a smoky mark
Of dread.
              Look upward. Neither firm nor free,

Purposeless matter hovers in the dark.

TRÄUMEREI

In this dream that dogs me I am part
Of a silent crowd walking under a wall,
Leaving a football match, perhaps, or a pit,
All moving the same way. After a while
A second wall closes on our right,
Pressing us tighter. We are now shut in
Like pigs down a concrete passage. When I lift
My head, I see the walls have killed the sun,
And light is cold. Now a giant whitewashed D
Comes on the second wall, but much too high
For them to recognise: I await the E,
Watch it approach and pass. By now
We have ceased walking and travel
Like water through sewers, steeply, despite
The tread that goes on ringing like an anvil
Under the striding A. I crook
My arm to shield my face, for we must pass
Beneath the huge, decapitated cross,
White on the wall, the T, and I cannot halt
The tread, the beat of it, it is my own heart,
The walls of my room rise, it is still night,
I have woken again before the word was spelt.

PHILIP LARKIN (1922–85)

THE DREAM

Or scorn, or pity on me take,
I must the true relation make:
      I am undone tonight;
  Love in a subtle dream disguised
  Hath both my heart and me surprised,
Whom never yet he durst attempt awake;
Nor will he tell me for whose sake
      He did me the delight,
        Or spite,
  But leaves me to inquire,
  In all my wild desire
    Of sleep again, who was his aid;
    And sleep so guilty and afraid
As, since, he dares not come within my sight.

THE DREAME

Deare love, for nothing lesse then thee
Would I have broke this happy dreame,
    It was a theame
For reason, much too strong for phantasie,
Therefore thou wakd'st me wisely; yet
My Dreame thou brok'st not, but continued'st it,
Thou art so truth, that thoughts of thee suffice,
To make dreames truths; and fables histories;
Enter these armes, for since thou thoughtst it best,
Not to dreame all my dreame, let's act the rest.

As lightning, or a Tapers light,
Thine eyes, and not thy noise wak'd mee;
    Yet I thought thee
(For thou lovest truth) an Angell, at first sight,
But when I saw thou sawest my heart,
And knew'st my thoughts, beyond an Angels art,
When thou knew'st what I dreamt, when thou knew'st
    when
Excess of joy would wake me, and cam'st then,
I must confesse, it could not chuse but bee
Prophane, to thinke thee any thing but thee.

Comming and staying show'd thee, thee,
But rising makes me doubt, that now,

    Thou art not thou.
That love is weake, where feare's as strong as hee;
'Tis not all spirit, pure, and brave,
If mixture it of *Feare, Shame, Honor,* have;
Perchance as torches which must ready bee,
Men light and put out, so thou deal'st with mee,
Thou cam'st to kindle, goest to come; Then I
Will dreame that hope againe, but else would die.

NIGHTMARES

DREAM

Last night I dreamt
This most strange dream,
And everywhere I saw
What did not seem could ever be:

You were not there with me!

Awake,
I turned
And touched you
Asleep,
Face to the wall.

I said,
How dreams
Can lie!

But you were not there at all!

SONGE D'ATHALIE
From Racine

It was a dream and shouldn't I bother about a dream?
But it goes on you know, tears me rather.
Of course I try to forget it but it will not let me.
Well it was on an extraordinarily dark night at midnight
My mother Queen Jezebel appeared suddenly before me
Looking just as she did the day she died, dressed
      grandly.
It was her pride you noticed, nothing she had gone
      through touched that
And she still had the look of being most carefully
      made up
She always made up a lot she didn't want people to
      know how old she was.
She spoke: Be warned my daughter, true girl to me,
      she said,
Do not suppose the cruel God of the Jews has finished
      with you,
I am come to weep your falling into his hands, my child.
With these appalling words my mother,
This ghost, leant over me stretching out her hands
And I stretched out my hands too to touch her
But what was it, oh this is horrible, what did I touch?
Nothing but the mangled flesh and the breaking bones
Of a body that the dogs tearing quarrelled over.

A DREAM OF CYNTHIA SHIPWRECKED

I saw you in a dream, my life, shipwrecked,
    Heaving weak hands through Ionian foam
And confessing all the lies you ever told me,
    Your sea-drenched hair weighing you down,
Like Helle tossing on the purple waves,
    Who rode the golden sheep's soft chine.

How scared I was lest the sea should bear your name
    And sailors gliding through your waters mourn you!
What then I vowed to Neptune, to Castor and his twin,
    And to the deified Leucóthoë!
But hardly lifting fingertips above the swell
    And almost gone you kept calling my name.

Had Glaucus caught sight of your eyes, you'd now
    Be an Ionian Sea-Nymph
And envious Nereids would criticize you,
    Nesaea fair, blue-eyed Cymóthoë.

But then I saw a dolphin speed to your support –
    The same, I fancy, as carried Arion's lyre;
And I was going to fling myself from the cliff-top
    When sheer fright shattered the vision for me.

PROPERTIUS (54/48–c. 16 B.C.)   141
TRANSLATED BY GUY LEE

THE OWL

What if to edge of dream,
When the spirit is come,
Shriek the hunting owl,
And summon it home –
To the fear-stirred heart
And the ancient dread
Of man, when cold root or stone
Pillowed roofless head?

Clangs not at last the hour
When roof shelters not;
And the ears are deaf,
And all fears forgot:
Since the spirit too far has fared
For summoning scream
Of any strange fowl on earth
To shatter its dream?

SLEEPING COMPARTMENT

I don't like this, being carried sideways
through the night. I feel wrong and helpless – like
a timber broadside in a fast stream.

Such a way of moving may suit
that odd snake the sidewinder
in Arizona: but not me in Perthshire.

I feel at rightangles to everything,
a crossgrain in existence. – It scrapes
the top of my head and my footsoles.

To forget outside is no help either –
then I become a blockage
in the long gut of the train.

I try to think I'm an Alice in Wonderland
mountaineer bivouacked
on a ledge five feet high.

It's no good. I go sidelong.
I rock sideways ... I draw in my feet
to let Aviemore pass.

NORMAN MacCAIG (1910–96)   143

GRATITUDE FOR A NIGHTMARE

His appearances are incalculable,
His strength terrible,
I do not know his name.

Huddling pensive for weeks on end, he
Gives only random hints of life, such as
Strokes of uncomfortable coincidence.

To eat heartily, dress warmly, lie snugly
And earn respect as a leading citizen
Granted long credit at all shops and inns –

How dangerous! I had feared this shag demon
Would not conform with my conformity
And in some leaner belly make his lair.

But now in dream he suddenly bestrides me. . . .
'All's well,' I groan, and fumble for a light,
Brow bathed in sweat, heart pounding.

THE NIGHTMARE

When you're lying awake with a dismal headache, and
     repose is taboo'd by anxiety,
I conceive you may use any language you choose to
     indulge in, without impropriety;
For your brain is on fire – the bedclothes conspire of
     usual slumber to plunder you:
First your counterpane goes, and uncovers your toes,
     and your sheet slips demurely from under you;
Then the blanketing tickles – you feel like mixed
     pickles – so terribly sharp is the pricking,
And you're hot, and you're cross, and you tumble and
     toss till there's nothing 'twixt you and the ticking.
Then the bedclothes all creep to the ground in a heap,
     and you pick 'em all up in a tangle;
Next your pillow resigns and politely declines to
     remain at its usual angle!
Well, you get some repose in the form of a doze, with
     hot eye-balls and head ever aching,
But your slumbering teems with such horrible dreams
     that you'd very much better be waking;
For you dream you are crossing the Channel, and
     tossing about in a steamer from Harwich –
Which is something between a large bathing machine
     and a very small second-class carriage –

And you're giving a treat (penny ice and cold meat) to
    a party of friends and relations –
They're a ravenous horde – and they all came on board
    at Sloane Square and South Kensington Stations.
And bound on that journey you find your attorney
    (who started that morning from Devon);
He's a bit undersized, and you don't feel surprised
    when he tells you he's only eleven.
Well, you're driving like mad with this singular lad
    (by-the-bye the ship's now a four-wheeler),
And you're playing round games, and he calls you bad
    names when you tell him that 'ties pay the dealer';
But this you can't stand, so you throw up your hand,
    and you find you're as cold as an icicle,
In your shirt and your socks (the black silk with gold
    clocks), crossing Salisbury Plain on a bicycle:
And he and the crew are on bicycles too – which
    they've somehow or other invested in –
And he's telling the tars, all the particu*lars* of a
    company he's interested in –
It's a scheme of devices, to get at low prices, all goods
    from cough mixtures to cables
(Which tickled the sailors) by treating retailers, as
    though they were all vege*ta*bles –
You get a good spadesman to plant a small tradesman,
    (first take off his boots with a boot-tree),
And his legs will take root, and his fingers will shoot,

and they'll blossom and bud like a fruit-tree –
From the greengrocer tree you get grapes and green
    pea, cauliflower, pineapple, and cranberries,
While the pastrycook plant, cherry brandy will grant,
    apple puffs, and three-corners, and banberries –
The shares are a penny, and ever so many are taken by
    Rothschild and Baring,
And just as a few are allotted to you, you awake with a
    shudder despairing –
You're a regular wreck, with a crick in your neck, and
    no wonder you snore, for your head's on the floor,
    and you've needles and pins from your soles to
    your shins, and your flesh is a-creep for your left
    leg's asleep, and you've cramp in your toes, and a
    fly on your nose, and some fluff in your lung, and a
    feverish tongue, and a thirst that's intense, and a
    general sense that you haven't been sleeping in
    clover;
But the darkness has passed, and it's daylight at last,
    and the night has been long – ditto ditto my
    song – and thank goodness they're both of them
    over!

THE DREAM

'What dreams you must have had last night,'
    My wife exclaims with a smile.
'Really, you threshed and muttered
    So loudly, for such a while

'I made up my mind to wake you.
    What was it you were dreaming?'
I yawn and stretch as I answer,
    'I can't remember a thing.

'What did I say?' 'Why, nothing –
    I couldn't make out a word.
You whimpered the way a puppy will.
    It was awfully absurd.'

I laugh and agree; and all the time
    The thought spins round in my head:
'If you'd guessed why I was crying
    Or what it was I said

'Would you too weep? or speak? or dream
    The dream that troubles me?
Does she know? What would she do?'
    And we smile uncertainly.

BAD DREAM

In my dream I was young and quick again –
High on the mountain-edge the villa stands –
Racing along the path there I ran down
And down, racing Ottilie, holding hands.

That little shape, so finely formed! The sweet
Twinkle of sea-green eyes, the fairy face . . .
She stands so firmly on her little feet,
Image of strength combined with daintiness.

Her voice rings true: each feeling syllable
Appears a contour of her soul in sound,
And all she says is wise and sensible:
Words that the rosebud lips are lifted round.

Something steals over me – not lover's pain,
This isn't raving; I've still got my sense –
But marvellously her nature weakens mine,
And shivering secretly I kiss her hands.

I think at last I picked a lily, gave
Her it, then gave the message out loud too:
'Ottilie, marry me and be my wife,
So I'll be good and happy just like you.'

But what her answer was, I never heard –
For suddenly I woke, and I was here
Again, a sick man in a sick man's bed,
Laid up and hopeless, for the umpteenth year.

150   HEINRICH HEINE (1797–1856)
TRANSLATED BY ALISTAIR ELLIOT

THE
INTERPRETATION
OF DREAMS

SONNET: A DREAM

The feeling tone was one of lost love,
bitter, as I woke with a cigar mouth;
but, as Bing Crosby and others have said and
sung, it's better, etc. You can't lose love
unless at one time, in some way, you had it.
As one grows older, one grows reconciled.
The names of the lost are at home in other beds
with difficulties of their own. Not including me.

Dreams work with a kind of neat backslang.
Love could be evol; and the boy a yob.
The approved thing is to be in love with Efil,
she's the girl you ought to fancy. She
is the warm abstraction books call positive.
I like her; but you couldn't call it love.

GAVIN EWART (1916–95)   153

WE DREAM

We dream – it is good we are dreaming –
It would hurt us – were we awake –
But since it is playing – kill us,
And we are playing – shriek –

What harm? Men die – externally –
It is a truth – of Blood –
But we – are dying in Drama –
And Drama – is never dead –

Cautious – We jar each other –
And either – open the eyes –
Lest the Phantasm – prove the Mistake –
And the livid Surprise

Cool us to Shafts of Granite –
With just an Age – and Name –
And perhaps a phrase in Egyptian –
It's prudenter – to dream –

From TO MADELEINE DE BROGLIE

... They tell us life's a dream; but that's not right.
It's not just dream. Dream too is a chaotic
fragment of life itself, within which sight
and being undisentanglably unite,
like golden animals, like those Nilotic
rulers brought out of crumbling death to light.

Dream is brocade that from yourself descends,
dream is a tree, a sound, a gleam that flies; —
a feeling that in you begins and ends
is dream; a beast that looks into your eyes
is dream; an angel that towards you bends
is dream. Dream is the word that seems to fall
into your feeling like the soft descent
of blossom on your hair: light, dazed, and spent, —
if you uplift your hands: then too comes dream,
comes into them like falling of a ball; —
almost all dreams, —
                              you, though, you bear it all.

You bear it all, and how it all enhances!
You're laden with it all as with your hair.
From depths below, from summits, it advances,
and by your favour it continues there ...

Where you are, nothing waits with unsuccess,
the things around you suffer no mischances.
I seem already to have been aware
of animals that bathed within your glances
and drank of your crystalline presentness.

But who you are I know not. Sing your praise
is all I can attain to: cyclic lays
around a soul,

        garden around a house,
within whose windows Heaven would appear. –
Oh, so much Heaven, attracting, from so near;
oh, so much Heaven over so much distance!

And when night falls: – what mighty stars' existence
must be reflected in those window-panes ...

TRANSLATED BY J. B. LEISHMAN

THE INTERPRETATION OF DREAMS

What animals dream of I do not know.
The urchin cat we rented with the house
was sun-stunned one minute and twitched

the next, pursued by humans, maybe.
The valley could be dreaming the haze
that filled it, both it and I

replete, like a wound
cat sleeping. The walled hilltowns
we drove to nights in search

of the perfect pasta also curled
in on themselves, like nutmeats.
How I loved those stone towns,

stark against fire, the houses
rising like tamed bluffs,
fortification as a way of life.

When I imagine an afternoon
nap in Gubbio, let's say, I dream
of light, mild cousin to fire,

bristling its blind rays
like a bottle-brush down house-
facades until they fleck the stony

streetbeds. Then I'd rise and walk
in diminishing circles *al centro*,
where there's a church and a square,

a blare of blank space amidst
all that habit and stricture.
How often I've arrived at myself

like that, as in a dream.
Nothing can be brought to an end
in the unconscious, where

the circuits of self-dramatization
complete themselves endlessly.
The dream-*work*, Freud called it,

'like fire*works* (my italics),
which require hours for their
preparation and then flare up

in a moment.' Daydreams like mine
of Gubbio imitate such
condensation and release,

though they lack that umbilical
tether to the other world that makes
dreams art and daydreams gossip.

And daydreams can be broken
off at sluggish will, like mine,
but dreams have their own urgencies.

The other night I dreamed
I was shaking myself awake
beside that waif cat, dead now

for two years. 'Let's go to Gubbio
tonight and eat tortellini.'
How long it takes to make them right,

and how they flare up
in the mouth like sunspots,
both dense and evanescent.

THE DIALECTIC OF DREAMS

Dream harbours Sin, and Innocence, and Magic,
re-stews mundane cabbage, stacks a shifting Tarot,
equivocates naïvely about Death, the secular
    Absolute –

things Rationality, the replacement aristocrat
approves only for enhancement. By midday
it has clarified its twinship with that relic –

but it comes round again, by deep night at the latest,
in a skin boat sailing on the blood
for dream lives its life engorged. It owns tumescence,

makes eerie conquests, can engender children –
though few who see the sun. The real takes some joint
    permission
and all of ourself not in the dream lies flaccid.

Every night, stepped mast or unfurled sail,
we reach a land where nothing is held trivial.

*

Real dreams are from home · back there. The light as
    it was,
will be, might have been · all the receding dream-tenses.

The dreamer is even yourself · or you're aware it is.
There in the action, unsafe · greater than the action,
  passive,

rarely uttering, in the endless · preparations, for
  horror, for happiness,
those appalling formulae · other-directed at us

which may persist as salt foam · on the margin of
  lapsed scenes
or, like the filmed cities, be resumed · into their own
  presence.

And that otherworld incongruence · spindling faintly
  through the day,
heightening thought, blanking it · silvering, beckoning
  away:

preternatural, those interiors · half-recalled by
  consciousness,
they were never in this world · not in your life, those
  wet bossed lanes.

Yet this is the heart of work · *the human sage, the butterfly*
to be conscious at the source of worlds · rapt, raising
  the ante.

*

The daylight oil, the heavier grade of Reason,
reverie's clear water, that of the dreamworld ocean
agitate us and are shaken, forming the emulsion

without which we make nothing much. Not art,
not love, not war, nor its reasoned nightmare methods,
not the Taj, not our homes, not the Masses or the gods

– but the fusion persists in the product, not in us.
A wheel shatters, drains our pooled rainbow. It was a
     moment:
the world is debris and museum of that moment,

its prospectus and farm. The wheel is turned by this
     engine.
I think of the people and buildings in a business street,
how they lack a perfect valve to take on and release

unceasing fusions. And will be pulled down for it,
their walls dreamed on in the milk of obsolete children.

*

Dream surrounds, is infused with this world. It is not
     subordinate.
We come from it; we live at tangents and accords with
     it; we go

back into it, at last, through the drowsing torture
    chambers to it.

We have gills for dream-life, in our head; we must keep
    them wet
from the nine-nights' immense, or dreams will emerge
    bodily, and enforce it.
Hide among or deny the shallow dreadful ones, and
    they may stay out:

moor things in Heaven and earth then, Ratio, anyhow
    you can
because dream's the looseleaf book, not of fiction, but
    of raw Pretend,
incalculable as this world when the God of Mercy
    intervened often.

It is the free splitting from God that parts Nature from
    dream.
They refresh each other with bafflement, each as the
    other's underground
freeing lives to be finite, because more; to be timeless,
    yet pure preparation –

while those spaces, sacred as the poor, of the haloed
    russet kingdom
are tigers impelling us, full of futures and pasts, toward
    a present.

SUNDAY, 4 A.M.

An endless and flooded
dreamland, lying low,
cross- and wheel-studded
like a tick-tack-toe.

At the right, ancillary,
'Mary''s close and blue.
Which Mary? Aunt Mary?
Tall Mary Stearns I knew?

The old kitchen knife box,
full of rusty nails,
is at the left. A high *vox
humana* somewhere wails:

*The gray horse needs shoeing!
It's always the same!
What are you doing,
there, beyond the frame?*

*If you're the donor,
you might do that much!*
Turn on the light. Turn over.
On the bed a smutch –

black-and-gold gesso
on the altered cloth.
The cat jumps to the window;
in his mouth's a moth.

DREAMS ARE THE
SUBTLE DOWER

Dreams are the subtle Dower
That make us rich an Hour –
Then fling us poor
Out of the purple Door
Into the Precinct raw
Possessed before –

INSOMNIA

COMPLAINT TO FOUR ANGELS

Every night at sleepy-time
Into bed I gladly climb.
Every night anew I hope
That with the covers I can cope.

Adjust the blanket fore and aft.
Swallow next a soothing draught;
Then a page of Scott or Cooper
May induce a healthful stupor.

O the soft luxurious dark,
Where carking cares no longer cark.
Traffic dies along the street.
The light is out. So are your feet.

Adjust the blanket aft and fore,
Sigh, and settle down once more.
Behold, a breeze! The curtains puff.
One blanket isn't quite enough.

Yawn and rise and seek your slippers,
Which, by now, are cold as kippers.
Yawn, and stretch, and prod yourself,
And fetch a blanket from the shelf.

And so to bed again, again,
Cozy under blankets twain.
Welcome warmth and sweet nirvana
Till eight o'clock or so mañana.

You sleep as deep as Crater Lake,
Then you dream and toss and wake.
Where is the breeze? There isn't any.
Two blankets, boy, are one too many.

O stilly night, why are you not
Consistent in your cold and hot?
O slumber's chains, unlocked so oft
With blankets being donned or doffed!

The angels who should guard my bed
I fear are slumbering instead.
O angels, please resume your hovering;
I'll sleep; and you adjust the covering.

TOSSING AND TURNING

The spirit has infinite facets, but the body confiningly
    few sides.
                There is the left,
the right, the back, the belly, and tempting
in-betweens, northeasts and northwests,
that tip the heart and soon pinch circulation
in one or another arm.
                  Yet we turn each time
with fresh hope, believing that sleep
will visit us here, descending like an angel
down the angle our flesh's sextant sets,
tilted toward that unreachable star
hung in the night between our eyebrows, whence
dreams and good luck flow.
                  Uncross
your ankles. Unclench your philosophy.
This bed was invented by others; know we go
to sleep less to rest than to participate
in the orthic twists of another world.
This churning is our journey.
                     It ends,
can only end, around a corner
we do not know
            we are turning.

JOHN UPDIKE (1932–)   171

BETTER THAN COUNTING SHEEP

For a night when sleep eludes you, I have,
At last, found the formula. Try to summon

All those ever known who are dead now, and soon
It will seem they are there in your room, not chairs
        enough

For the party, or standing space even, the hall
Chock-full, and faces thrust to the pane to peer.

Then somehow the house, in a wink, isn't there,
But a field full of folk, and some,

Those near, touch your sleeve, so sadly and slow,
        and all
Want something of you, too timid to ask – and you
        don't

Know what. Yes, even in distance and dimness, hands
Are out – stretched to glow faintly

Like fox-fire in marshland where deadfall
Rots, though a few trunks unsteadily stand.

Meanwhile, in the grieving susurrus, all wordless,
You sense, at last, what they want. Each,

Male or female, young or age-gnawed, beloved or not –
Each wants to know if you remember a name.

But now you can't answer, not even your mother's
      name, and your heart
Howls with the loneliness of a wolf in

The depth of a snow-throttled forest when the moon,
      full,
Spills the spruce-shadows African black. Then you are,
      suddenly,

Alone. And your own name gone, as you plunge in ink-
      shadow or snowdrift.
The shadows are dreams – but of what? And the
      snowdrift, sleep.

TO HIS WATCH, WHEN HE COULD NOT SLEEP

Uncessant Minutes, whil'st you move you tell
    The time that tells our life, which though it run
    Never so fast or farr, your new begun
Short steps shall overtake; for though life well

May scape his own Account, it shall not yours,
    You are Death's Auditors, that both divide
And summ what ere that life inspir'd endures
    Past a beginning, and through you we bide

The doom of Fate, whose unrecall'd Decree
    You date, bring, execute; making what's new,
Ill and good, old, for as we die in you,
    You die in Time, Time in Eternity.

NEVERTHELESS THE MOON

Nevertheless the moon
Heightens the secret
Sleep long withheld
Dry for a rain of dreams –
Flies straight above me
White, hot-hearted,
Among the streaming
Firmament armies.
A monk of flames
Stands shaking in my heart
Where sleep might lie.

Where you all night have lain.
And now hang dreaming,
Faded acute, fade full,
Calling your cloudy fame,
A keen high nightlong cry.
Rises my silent, turning
Heart. Heart where my love
Might lie, try toward my love
Flying, let go all need,
Brighten and burn –
Rain down, raging for life
Light my love's dream tonight.

MURIEL RUKEYSER (1913–80)

INSOMNIA

Insomnia. Homer. Tautly swelling sails.
I've read the catalogue of ships half through:
This wedge of cranes, this outstretched brood
That once took wing across the Aegean isles.

A train of cranes outstretched towards alien frontiers,
The foam of gods crowns the leaders' kingly hair.
Where sail you to? If Helen were not there,
What would Troy mean for you, oh warriors of
    Greece?

Both Homer and the sea: all things are moved by love;
To whom shall I pay heed? Homer here is silent
And the dark sea thunders, eloquent,
And rumbling heavily, it breaks beneath my bed.

TRANSLATED BY BERNARD MEARES

INSOMNIA

The moon in the bureau mirror
looks out a million miles
(and perhaps with pride, at herself,
but she never, never smiles)
far and away beyond sleep, or
perhaps she's a daytime sleeper.

By the Universe deserted,
she'd tell it to go to hell,
and she'd find a body of water,
or a mirror, on which to dwell.
So wrap up care in a cobweb
and drop it down the well

into that world inverted
where left is always right,
where the shadows are really the body,
where we stay awake all night,
where the heavens are shallow as the sea
is now deep, and you love me.

VIBRATION

The world vibrates, my sleepless nights
discovered. The air conditioner hummed;
I turned it off. The plumbing
in the next apartment sang;
I moved away, and found a town
whose factories shuddered as they worked
all night. The wires on the poles
outside my windows quivered in an ecstasy
stretched thin between horizons.
I went to where no wires were; and there,
as I lay still, a dragon tremor
seized my darkened body, gnawed
my heart, and murmured, *I am you.*

From INSOMNIA

After a sleepless night the body weakens.
It grows dear, not one's own, it's nobody's.
Sluggish, the veins still retain an ache of arrows,
One smiles to all with a seraph's ease.

After a sleepless night the hands weaken.
Deeply indifferent are both friend and enemy.
Each casual sound contains an entire rainbow.
And the frost smells of Florence suddenly.

Lips glow softly, the shadow's more golden
Under sunken eyes. Night has set ablaze
This most radiant countenance – and dark night renders
But one part of us dark – the eyes.

MARINA TSVETAEVA (1892–1941)   179
TRANSLATED BY DAVID McDUFF

SAPPHICS

All the night sleep came not upon my eyelids,
Shed not dew, nor shook nor unclosed a feather,
Yet with lips shut close and with eyes of iron
    Stood and beheld me.

Then to me so lying awake a vision
Came without sleep over the seas and touched me,
Softly touched mine eyelids and lips; and I too,
    Full of the vision,

Saw the white implacable Aphrodite,
Saw the hair unbound and the feet unsandalled
Shine as fire of sunset on western waters;
    Saw the reluctant

Feet, the straining plumes of the doves that drew her,
Looking always, looking with necks reverted,
Back to Lesbos, back to the hills whereunder
    Shone Mitylene;

Heard the flying feet of the Loves behind her
Make a sudden thunder upon the waters,
As the thunder flung from the strong unclosing
    Wings of a great wind.

So the goddess fled from her place, with awful
Sound of feet and thunder of wings around her;
While behind a clamour of singing women
    Severed the twilight.

Ah the singing, ah the delight, the passion!
All the Loves wept, listening; sick with anguish,
Stood the crowned nine Muses about Apollo;
    Fear was upon them,

While the tenth sang wonderful things they knew not.
Ah the tenth, the Lesbian! the nine were silent,
None endured the sound of her song for weeping;
    Laurel by laurel,

Faded all their crowns; but about her forehead,
Round her woven tresses and ashen temples
White as dead snow, paler than grass in summer,
    Ravaged with kisses,

Shone a light of fire as a crown for ever.
Yea, almost the implacable Aphrodite
Paused, and almost wept; such a song was that song.
    Yea, by her name too

Called her, saying, 'Turn to me, O my Sappho';
Yet she turned her face from the Loves, she saw not
Tears for laughter darken immortal eyelids,
    Heard not about her

Fearful fitful wings of the doves departing,
Saw not how the bosom of Aphrodite
Shook with weeping, saw not her shaken raiment,
    Saw not her hands wrung;

Saw the Lesbians kissing across their smitten
Lutes with lips more sweet than the sound of lute-
        strings,
Mouth to mouth and hand upon hand, her chosen,
    Fairer than all men;

Only saw the beautiful lips and fingers,
Full of songs and kisses and little whispers,
Full of music; only beheld among them
    Soar, as a bird soars

Newly fledged, her visible song, a marvel,
Made of perfect sound and exceeding passion,
Sweetly shapen, terrible, full of thunders,
    Clothed with the wind's wings.

Then rejoiced she, laughing with love, and scattered
Roses, awful roses of holy blossom;
Then the Loves thronged sadly with hidden faces
   Round Aphrodite,

Then the Muses, stricken at heart, were silent;
Yea, the gods waxed pale; such a song was that song.
All reluctant, all with a fresh repulsion,
   Fled from before her.

All withdrew long since, and the land was barren,
Full of fruitless women and music only.
Now perchance, when winds are assuaged at sunset,
   Lulled at the dewfall,

By the grey sea-side, unassuaged, unheard of,
Unbeloved, unseen in the ebb of twilight,
Ghosts of outcast women return lamenting,
   Purged not in Lethe,

Clothed about with flame and with tears, and singing
Songs that move the heart of the shaken heaven,
Songs that break the heart of the earth with pity,
   Hearing, to hear them.

INSOMNIA

Insomnia, impalpable Animal!
Is your love only cerebral?
That you come and are delighted to spy,
Under your evil eye, the man chewing
His sheets, writhing and stewing
With ennui! ... Under your black diamond eye.

Tell me: why, in a night without repose,
Rainy like a Sunday, in you lope
To lick us like a dog: Hope
Or Regret keeping watch, close
At our ear throbbing
You speak low ... and say nothing?

Why do you always pass
To our parched throats your empty glass
And leave us with our necks contorted,
Tantaluses, drunkards on chimera:
– Bitter dregs or loving philtre,
Cool dew or molten lead! –

Insomnia, aren't you a pretty miss? ...
Well why, lewd maid,
Do you get us between your hips?
Why fade out on our lips,

Why leave our bed unmade
And ... don't get laid?

Why, Pretty-by-night, blooming unclean,
This black mask on your face? ...
– To complicate golden dreams? ...
Aren't you love in space,
The breath of Messalina, exhausted,
But not yet sated!

Insomnia, are you Hysteria ...
Are you the barrel organ grinding
The Elect's *Hosannah*? ...
– Or aren't you the plectrum everlasting
On the nerves of the damned-of-letters, who tone
Up verses – read by them alone.

Insomnia, are you Buridan's
Ass in turmoil – or the moth
Of hell? – Your fiery kiss fans
A cold taste of iron red-hot ...
Oh! come to my hovel and settle! ...
We'll sleep together a little.

TRISTAN CORBIÈRE (1845–75)
TRANSLATED BY VAL WARNER   185

NOT TO SLEEP

Not to sleep all the night long, for pure joy,
Counting no sheep and careless of chimes,
Welcoming the dawn confabulation
Of birds, her children, who discuss idly
Fanciful details of the promised coming –
Will she be wearing red, or russet, or blue,
Or pure white? – whatever she wears, glorious:
Not to sleep all the night long, for pure joy,
This is given to few but at last to me,
So that when I laugh and stretch and leap from bed
I shall glide downstairs, my feet brushing the carpet
In courtesy to civilized progression,
Though, did I wish, I could soar through the open
      window
And perch on a branch above, acceptable ally
Of the birds still alert, grumbling gently together.

I WAKE AND FEEL

I wake and feel the fell of dark, not day.
What hours, O what black hoúrs we have spent
This night! what sights you, heart, saw; ways you
    went!
And more must, in yet longer light's delay.

With witness I speak this. But where I say
Hours I mean years, mean life. And my lament
Is cries countless, cries like dead letters sent
To dearest him that lives alas! away.

I am gall, I am heartburn. God's most deep decree
Bitter would have me taste: my taste was me;
Bones built in me, flesh filled, blood brimmed the
    curse.

Selfyeast of spirit a dull dough sours. I see
The lost are like this, and their scourge to be,
As I am mine, their sweating selves; but worse.

IF THIS ROOM IS OUR WORLD

If this room is our world, then let
This world be damned. Open this roof
For one last monstrous flood
To sweep away this floor, these chairs,
This bed that takes me to no sleep.
Under the black sky of our circumstance,
Mumbling of wet barometers, I stare
At citied dust that soils the glass
While thunder perishes. The heroes perish
Miles from here. Their blood runs heavy in the grass,
Sweet, restless, clotted, sickening,
Runs to the rivers and the seas, the seas
That are the source of that devouring flood
That I await, that I must perish by.

INSOMNIAC

The night sky is only a sort of carbon paper,
Blueblack, with the much-poked periods of stars
Letting in the light, peephole after peephole –
A bonewhite light, like death, behind all things.
Under the eyes of the stars and the moon's rictus
He suffers his desert pillow, sleeplessness
Stretching its fine, irritating sand in all directions.

Over and over the old, granular movie
Exposes embarrassments – the mizzling days
Of childhood and adolescence, sticky with dreams,
Parental faces on tall stalks, alternately stern and
    tearful,
A garden of buggy roses that made him cry.
His forehead is bumpy as a sack of rocks.
Memories jostle each other for face-room like obsolete
    film stars.

He is immune to pills: red, purple, blue –
How they lit the tedium of the protracted evening!
Those sugary planets whose influence won for him
A life baptized in no-life for a while,
And the sweet, drugged waking of a forgetful baby.
Now the pills are worn-out and silly, like classical gods.
Their poppy-sleepy colors do him no good.

His head is a little interior of gray mirrors.
Each gesture flees immediately down an alley
Of diminishing perspectives, and its significance
Drains like water out the hole at the far end.
He lives without privacy in a lidless room,
The bald slots of his eyes stiffened wide-open
On the incessant heat-lightning flicker of situations.

Nightlong, in the granite yard, invisible cats
Have been howling like women, or damaged
        instruments.
Already he can feel daylight, his white disease,
Creeping up with her hatful of trivial repetitions.
The city is a map of cheerful twitters now,
And everywhere people, eyes mica-silver and blank,
Are riding to work in rows, as if recently brainwashed.

IS IT THY WILL

Is it thy will thy image should keep open
My heavy eyelids to the weary night?
Dost thou desire my slumbers should be broken
While shadows like to thee do mock my sight?
Is it thy spirit that thou send'st from thee
So far from home into my deeds to pry,
To find out shames and idle hours in me,
The scope and tenure of thy jealousy?
O no, thy love, though much, is not so great.
It is my love that keeps mine eye awake,
Mine own true love that doth my rest defeat,
To play the watchman ever for thy sake.
    For thee watch I, whilst thou dost wake elsewhere,
    From me far off, with others all too near.

WILLIAM SHAKESPEARE (1564–1616)   191

INSOMNIA
Necropolis of Pantàlica

A happy wafting of winged
creatures at odds with green light;
the sea in the leaves.

I am out of tune. And time
rends all that is born to joy in me;
keeps scarcely its echo in voice of trees.

Love for me lost,
memory not human; celestial
stigmata shine on the dead,
starred bodies fall in the rivers;
an hour grows hoarse with gentle rain,
or stirs a song in this eternal night.

For years and years I have been asleep
in an open cell of my land,
shoulders of seaweed against grey waters:

meteors thunder in the unmoving air.

NIGHT THOUGHTS

THE BENCH OF BOORS

In bed I muse on Teniers' boors,
Embrowned and beery losels all:
     A wakeful brain
     Elaborates pain:
Within low doors the slugs of boors
Laze and yawn and doze again.

In dreams they doze, the drowsy boors,
Their hazy hovel warm and small:
     Thought's ampler bound
     But chill is found:
Within low doors the basking boors
Snugly hug the ember-mound.

Sleepless, I see the slumberous boors
Their blurred eyes blink, their eyelids fall:
     Thought's eager sight
     Aches – overbright!
Within low doors the boozy boors
Cat-naps take in pipe-bowl light.

HERMAN MELVILLE (1819–91)

STARS

Ah! why, because the dazzling sun
    Restored our Earth to joy,
Have you departed, every one,
    And left a desert sky?

All through the night, your glorious eyes
    Were gazing down in mine,
And with a full heart's thankful sighs,
    I blessed that watch divine.

I was at peace, and drank your beams
    As they were life to me;
And revelled in my changeful dreams,
    Like petrel on the sea.

Thought followed thought, star followed star,
    Through boundless regions, on;
While one sweet influence, near and far,
    Thrilled through, and proved us one!

Why did the morning dawn to break
    So great, so pure, a spell;
And scorch with fire, the tranquil cheek,
    Where your cool radiance fell?

Blood-red, he rose, and, arrow-straight,
    His fierce beams struck my brow;
The soul of nature, sprang, elate,
    But *mine* sank sad and low!

My lids closed down, yet through their veil,
    I saw him, blazing, still,
And steep in gold the misty dale,
    And flash upon the hill.

I turned me to the pillow, then,
    To call back night, and see
Your worlds of solemn light, again,
    Throb with my heart, and me!

It would not do – the pillow glowed,
    And glowed both roof and floor;
And birds sang loudly in the wood,
    And fresh winds shook the door;

The curtains waved, the wakened flies
    Were murmuring round my room,
Imprisoned there, till I should rise,
    And give them leave to roam.

Oh, stars, and dreams, and gentle night;
    Oh, night and stars return!
And hide me from the hostile light,
    That does not warm, but burn;

That drains the blood of suffering men;
    Drinks tears, instead of dew;
Let me sleep through his blinding reign,
    And only wake with you!

EMILY BRONTË (1818–48)

THOUGHTS IN NIGHT QUIET

Seeing moonlight here at my bed,
and thinking it's frost on the ground,

I look up, gaze at the mountain moon,
then back, dreaming of my old home.

LI PO (701–62)
    TRANSLATED BY DAVID HINTON

FROST AT MIDNIGHT

The Frost performs its secret ministry,
Unhelped by any wind. The owlet's cry
Came loud – and hark, again! loud as before.
The inmates of my cottage, all at rest,
Have left me to that solitude, which suits
Abstruser musings: save that at my side
My cradled infant slumbers peacefully.
'Tis calm indeed! so calm, that it disturbs
And vexes meditation with its strange
And extreme silentness. Sea, hill, and wood,
This populous village! Sea, and hill, and wood,
With all the numberless goings-on of life,
Inaudible as dreams! the thin blue flame
Lies on my low-burnt fire, and quivers not;
Only that film, which fluttered on the grate,
Still flutters there, the sole unquiet thing.
Methinks, its motion in this hush of nature
Gives it dim sympathies with me who live,
Making it a companionable form,
Whose puny flaps and freaks the idling Spirit
By its own moods interprets, every where
Echo or mirror seeking of itself,
And makes a toy of Thought.

                              But O! how oft,
How oft, at school, with most believing mind,

Presageful, have I gazed upon the bars,
To watch that fluttering *stranger*! and as oft
With unclosed lids, already had I dreamt
Of my sweet birth-place, and the old church-tower,
Whose bells, the poor man's only music, rang
From morn to evening, all the hot Fair-day,
So sweetly, that they stirred and haunted me
With a wild pleasure, falling on mine ear
Most like articulate sounds of things to come!
So gazed I, till the soothing things, I dreamt,
Lulled me to sleep, and sleep prolonged my dreams!
And so I brooded all the following morn,
Awed by the stern preceptor's face, mine eye
Fixed with mock study on my swimming book:
Save if the door half opened, and I snatched
A hasty glance, and still my heart leaped up,
For still I hoped to see the *stranger's* face,
Townsman, or aunt, or sister more beloved,
My play-mate when we both were clothed alike!

Dear Babe, that sleepest cradled by my side,
Whose gentle breathings, heard in this deep calm,
Fill up the interspersèd vacancies
And momentary pauses of the thought!
My babe so beautiful! it thrills my heart
With tender gladness, thus to look at thee,
And think that thou shalt learn far other lore,

And in far other scenes! For I was reared
In the great city, pent 'mid cloisters dim,
And saw nought lovely but the sky and stars.
But *thou*, my babe! shalt wander like a breeze
By lakes and sandy shores, beneath the crags
Of ancient mountain, and beneath the clouds,
Which image in their bulk both lakes and shores
And mountain crags: so shalt thou see and hear
The lovely shapes and sounds intelligible
Of that eternal language, which thy God
Utters, who from eternity doth teach
Himself in all, and all things in himself.
Great universal Teacher! he shall mould
Thy spirit, and by giving make it ask.

Therefore all seasons shall be sweet to thee,
Whether the summer clothe the general earth
With greenness, or the redbreast sit and sing
Betwixt the tufts of snow on the bare branch
Of mossy apple-tree, while the nigh thatch
Smokes in the sun-thaw; whether the eave-drops fall
Heard only in the trances of the blast,
Or if the secret ministry of frost
Shall hang them up in silent icicles,
Quietly shining to the quiet Moon.

I CAN HARDLY WAIT FOR THE SANDMAN

There are several differences between me and Samuel
    Taylor Coleridge, whose bust I stand admiringly
    beneath;
He found solace in opium, I found it in Codman's Bay-
    berry Chewing Gum, at least until it started
    loosening my teeth.
Another difference between me and Samuel Taylor
    Coleridge is more massive in design:
People used to interrupt him while he was dreaming his
    dreams, but they interrupt me while I am recount-
    ing mine.
Now, if anybody buttonholes you to tell you about how
    they dreamt they were falling, or flying, or just
    about to die and they actually would have died if
    they hadn't woken up abruptly,
Well, they deserve to be treated interruptly,
But when somebody with a really interesting dream
    takes the floor,
I don't think people ought to break away and start
    listening to the neighborhood bore.
Therefore I feel I need offer no apology
For having gathered a few of my more representative
    dreams into a modest anthology.
Once I dreamt I was in this sort of, you know, desert
    with cactuses only they were more like caterpillars
    and there were skulls and all the rest,

And right in the middle of this desert was a lifeboat
      with the name *Mary Celeste*,
And if I hadn't woken up because the heat was so
      blistery,
Why, I bet I would have solved this mystery of nautical
      history.
Another time I dreamt I was climbing this mountain
      although actually it was more like a beach,
And all of a sudden this sort of a merry-go-round I
      forgot to tell you about turned into a shack with a
      sign saying, LEDA'S PLACE, SWANBURGERS 10¢ EACH.
I hope you will agree that of dreams I am a connoisseur,
And next time I will tell you about either how I dreamt
      I went down the rabbit hole or through the looking
      glass, whichever you prefer.

OGDEN NASH (1902–71)   203

WHEN I HEARD AT THE CLOSE
OF THE DAY

When I heard at the close of the day how my name had
      been receiv'd with plaudits in the capitol, still it
      was not a happy night for me that follow'd,
And else when I carous'd, or when my plans were
      accomplish'd, still I was not happy,
But the day when I rose at dawn from the bed of
      perfect health, refresh'd, singing, inhaling the ripe
      breath of autumn,
When I saw the full moon in the west grow pale and
      disappear in the morning light,
When I wander'd alone over the beach, and undressing
      bathed, laughing with the cool waters, and saw
      the sun rise,
And when I thought how my dear friend my lover was
      on his way coming, O then I was happy,
O then each breath tasted sweeter, and all that day my
      food nourish'd me more, and the beautiful day
      pass'd well,
And the next came with equal joy, and with the next at
      evening came my friend,
And that night while all was still I heard the waters
      roll slowly continually up the shores,
I heard the hissing rustle of the liquid and sands as
      directed to me whispering to congratulate me,

For the one I love most lay sleeping by me under the
    same cover in the cool night,
In the stillness in the autumn moonbeams his face was
    inclined toward me,
And his arm lay lightly around my breast – and that
    night I was happy.

PILLOW

Plump mate to my head, you alone absorb,
through your cotton skin, the thoughts behind
    my bone
skin of skull. When I weep, you grow damp.
When I turn, you comply. In the dark,
you are my only friend, the only kiss
my cheek receives. You are my bowl of dreams.
Your underside is cool, like a second chance,
like a little leap into the air when I turn
you over. Though you would smother me,
properly applied, you are, like the world
with its rotating mass, all I have. You accept
the strange night with me, and are depressed
when the morning discloses your wrinkles.

SLEEP IN THE MOJAVE DESERT

Out here there are no hearthstones,
Hot grains, simply. It is dry, dry.
And the air dangerous. Noonday acts queerly
On the mind's eye, erecting a line
Of poplars in the middle distance, the only
Object beside the mad, straight road
One can remember men and houses by.
A cool wind should inhabit those leaves
And a dew collect on them, dearer than money,
In the blue hour before sunup.
Yet they recede, untouchable as tomorrow,
Or those glittery fictions of spilt water
That glide ahead of the very thirsty.

I think of the lizards airing their tongues
In the crevice of an extremely small shadow
And the toad guarding his heart's droplet.
The desert is white as a blind man's eye,
Comfortless as salt. Snake and bird
Doze behind the old masks of fury.
We swelter like firedogs in the wind.
The sun puts its cinder out. Where we lie
The heat-cracked crickets congregate
In their black armorplate and cry.
The day-moon lights up like a sorry mother,
And the crickets come creeping into our hair
To fiddle the short night away.

SYLVIA PLATH (1932–63)   207

A GOODNIGHT

Go to sleep – though of course you will not –
to tideless waves thundering slantwise against
strong embankments, rattle and swish of spray
dashed thirty feet high, caught by the lake wind,
scattered and strewn broadcast in over the steady
car rails! Sleep, sleep! Gulls' cries in a wind-gust
broken by the wind; calculating wings set above
the field of waves breaking.
Go to sleep to the lunge between foam-crests,
refuse churned in the recoil. Food! Food!
Offal! Offal! that holds them in the air, wave-white
for the one purpose, feather upon feather, the wild
chill in their eyes, the hoarseness in their voices –
sleep, sleep . . .

Gentlefooted crowds are treading out your lullaby.
Their arms nudge, they brush shoulders,
hitch this way then that, mass and surge at the
    crossings –
lullaby, lullaby! The wild-fowl police whistles,
the enraged roar of the traffic, machine shrieks:
it is all to put you to sleep,
to soften your limbs in relaxed postures,
and that your head slip sidewise, and your hair loosen
and fall over your eyes and over your mouth,

208

brushing your lips wistfully that you may dream,
sleep and dream –

A black fungus springs out about lonely church doors –
sleep, sleep. The Night, coming down upon
the wet boulevard, would start you awake with his
message, to have in at your window. Pay no
heed to him. He storms at your sill with
cooings, with gesticulations, curses!
You will not let him in. He would keep you from
        sleeping.
He would have you sit under your desk lamp
brooding, pondering; he would have you
slide out the drawer, take up the ornamented dagger
and handle it. It is late, it is nineteen-nineteen –
go to sleep, his cries are a lullaby;
his jabbering is a sleep-well-my-baby; he is
a crackbrained messenger.

The maid waking you in the morning
when you are up and dressing,
the rustle of your clothes as you raise them –
it is the same tune.
At table the cold, greenish, split grapefruit, its juice
on the tongue, the clink of the spoon in
your coffee, the toast odors say it over and over.

The open street-door lets in the breath of
the morning wind from over the lake.
The bus coming to a halt grinds from its sullen
        brakes –
lullaby, lullaby. The crackle of a newspaper,
the movement of the troubled coat beside you –
sleep, sleep, sleep, sleep . . .
It is the sting of snow, the burning liquor of
the moonlight, the rush of rain in the gutters packed
with dead leaves: go to sleep, go to sleep.
And the night passes – and never passes –

AN OLD MAN

In the inner room of the noisy café
an old man sits bent over a table;
a newspaper before him, no companion beside him.

And in the scorn of his miserable old age,
he meditates how little he enjoyed the years
when he had strength, the art of the word, and good
      looks.

He knows he has aged much; he is aware of it, he sees it,
and yet the time when he was young seems like
yesterday. How short a time, how short a time.

And he ponders how Wisdom had deceived him;
and how he always trusted her – what folly! –
the liar who would say, 'Tomorrow. You have ample
      time.'

He recalls impulses he curbed; and how much
joy he sacrificed. Every lost chance
now mocks his senseless prudence.

... But with so much thinking and remembering
the old man reels. And he dozes off
bent over the table of the café.

C. P. CAVAFY (1863–1933)   211

AUBADE

MOONRISE

I awoke in the Midsummer not-to-call night, in the
    white and the walk of the morning:
The moon, dwindled and thinned to the fringe of a
    fingernail held to the candle,
Or paring of paradisaïcal fruit, lovely in waning but
    lustreless,
Stepped from the stool, drew back from the barrow, of
    dark Maenefa the mountain;
A cusp still clasped him, a fluke yet fanged him,
    entangled him, not quit utterly.
This was the prized, the desirable sight, unsought,
    presented so easily,
Parted me leaf and leaf, divided me, eyelid and eyelid of
    slumber.

GERARD MANLEY HOPKINS (1844–89)

THE EARLY MORNING

The moon on the one hand, the dawn on the other:
The moon is my sister, the dawn is my brother.
The moon on my left and the dawn on my right.
My brother, good morning: my sister, good night.

HILAIRE BELLOC (1870–1953)   215

THE HORNS OF THE MORNING

The horns of the morning
Are blowing, are shining,
The meadows are bright
   With the coldest dew;
The dawn reassembles,
Like the clash of gold cymbals
The sky spreads its vans out
   The sun hangs in view.

Here, where no love is,
All that was hopeless
And kept me from sleeping
   Is frail and unsure;
For never so brilliant,
Neither so silent
Nor so unearthly, has
   Earth grown before.

JULY DAWN

It was a waning crescent
Dark on the wrong side
On which one does not wish
Setting in the hour before daylight
For my sleepless eyes to look at.

O, as a symbol of dis-hope
Over the July fields,
Dissolving, waning.
In spite of its sickle shape.

I saw it and thought it new
In that short moment
That makes all symbols lucky
Before we read them rightly.

Down to the dark it swam,
Down to the dark it moved,
Swift to that cluster of evenings
When curved toward the full it sharpens.

LOUISE BOGAN (1897–1970)   217

DEAR, THOUGH THE NIGHT IS GONE

Dear, though the night is gone,
The dream still haunts to-day
That brought us to a room,
Cavernous, lofty as
A railway terminus,
And crowded in that gloom
Were beds, and we in one
In a far corner lay.

Our whisper woke no clocks,
We kissed and I was glad
At everything you did,
Indifferent to those
Who sat with hostile eyes
In pairs on every bed,
Arms round each other's necks,
Inert and vaguely sad.

O but what worm of guilt
Or what malignant doubt
Am I the victim of;
That you then, unabashed,
Did what I never wished,
Confessed another love;
And I, submissive, felt
Unwanted and went out?

218   W. H. AUDEN (1907–73)

SOMETHING SAID, WAKING DRUNK ON A SPRING DAY

It's like boundless dream here in this
world, nothing anywhere to trouble us.

I have, therefore, been drunk all day,
a shambles of sleep on the front porch.

Coming to, I look into the courtyard.
There's a bird among blossoms calling,

and when I ask what season this is,
an oriole's voice drifts on spring winds.

Overcome, verging on sorrow and lament,
I pour another drink. Soon, awaiting

this bright moon, I'm chanting a song.
And now it's over, I've forgotten why.

LI PO (701–62)   219
TRANSLATED BY DAVID HINTON

MORNING AFTER

I was so sick last night I
Didn't hardly know my mind.
So sick last night I
Didn't know my mind.
I drunk some bad licker that
Almost made me blind.

Had a dream last night I
Thought I was in hell.
I drempt last night I
Thought I was in hell.
Woke up and looked around me –
Babe, your mouth was open like a well.

I said, Baby! Baby!
Please don't snore so loud.
Baby! Please!
Please don't snore so loud.
You jest a little bit o' woman but you
Sound like a great big crowd.

From HORAE CANONICAE
'Immolatus vicerit'

PRIME

Simultaneously, as soundlessly,
  Spontaneously, suddenly
As, at the vaunt of the dawn, the kind
  Gates of the body fly open
To its world beyond, the gates of the mind,
  The horn gate and the ivory gate,
Swing to, swing shut, instantaneously
  Quell the nocturnal rummage
Of its rebellious fronde, ill-favored,
  Ill-natured and second-rate,
Disenfranchised, widowed and orphaned
  By an historical mistake:
Recalled from the shades to be a seeing being,
  From absence to be on display,
Without a name or history I wake
  Between my body and the day.

Holy this moment, wholly in the right,
  As, in complete obedience
To the light's laconic outcry, next
  As a sheet, near as a wall,
Out there as a mountain's poise of stone,
  The world is present, about,

And I know that I am, here, not alone
    But with a world, and rejoice
Unvexed, for the will has still to claim
    This adjacent arm as my own,
The memory to name me, resume
    Its routine of praise and blame,
And smiling to me is this instant while
    Still the day is intact, and I
The Adam sinless in our beginning,
    Adam still previous to any act.

I draw breath; that is of course to wish
    No matter what, to be wise,
To be different, to die and the cost,
    No matter how, is Paradise
Lost of course and myself owing a death:
    The eager ridge, the steady sea,
The flat roofs of the fishing village
    Still asleep in its bunny,
Though as fresh and sunny still, are not friends
    But things to hand, this ready flesh
No honest equal but my accomplice now,
    My assassin to be, and my name
Stands for my historical share of care
    For a lying self-made city,
Afraid of our living task, the dying
    Which the coming day will ask.

MORNING

'Tis the hour when white-horsed Day
    Chases Night her mares away,
When the Gates of Dawn (they say)
    Phoebus opes:
And I gather that the Queen
May be uniformly seen,
Should the weather be serene,
    On the slopes.

When the ploughman, as he goes
Leathern-gaitered o'er the snows,
From his hat and from his nose
    Knocks the ice;
And the panes are frosted o'er
And the lawn is crisp and hoar.
As has been observed before
    Once or twice.

When arrayed in breastplate red
Sings the robin, for his bread,
On the elmtree that hath shed
    Every leaf;
While, within, the frost benumbs
The still sleepy schoolboy's thumbs,
And in consequence his sums
    Come to grief.

But when breakfast-time hath come,
And he's crunching crust and crumb,
He'll no longer look a glum
    Little dunce;
But be as brisk as bees that settle
On a summer rose's petal:
Wherefore, Polly, put the kettle
    On at once.

AUBADE

Now all those onward-going,
far-faring plans resurge.
Outside the cocks are crowing:
distance must re-emerge

after all the nearness
which so enfolded us.
Now let me see that dearness
that felt so rapturous.

Still through my blood it's coursing,
the house still holds the scent.
To, oh, what sweet discoursing
my mouth to yours was bent,

on your kind mouth was lying,
on your reposeful breast:
hour after hour went flying
above us all unguessed.

Louder the sounds are getting,
a door has opened there.
To mitigate regretting,
wake with me, feel aware

how day's voice ever firmer
tells us to say adieu –
Waken to me and murmur:
Do I look sad to you?

Not long you'll have to bear it,
the pain will soon have ceased.
Night comes that we may share it,
day's here to be increased.

226   R. M. RILKE (1875–1926)
TRANSLATED BY J. B. LEISHMAN

EARLY RISING

I arose early, O my true love!
I was awake and wide
To see the last star quenched above
And the moon lying on her side.

I saw the tops of the tall elms shine
Over the mist on the lea,
And the new bells upon the bine
Opened most silently;
And in the foggy dew the kine
Lay still as rocks in the sea.

The foggy dew lay on the flower
Silver and soft and chaste:
The turtle in her oaken tower
To waken made no haste:
Slept by her love another hour
And her two young embraced.

Mine was the solemn silence then,
And that clean tract of sky:
There was no smoke from hearths of men,
As yet no one went by:
The beast of night had sought his den,
The lark not climbed on high.

It was an hour of Eden; yea,
So still the time and slow,
I thought the sun mistook his way,
And was bewildered so
That coming he might bring a day
Lost since a thousand years ago:

A day of innocence and mirth,
A birds' day, day of prayer,
When every simple tongue on earth
A song or psalm might bear:
When love of God was something worth,
And holiness not killed with care.

But even while musing so, I laid
Flame to the gathered wood:
The sullying smoke swept up the glade,
Abashed the morning stood:
And in the mead the milking-maid
Called up the kine with accents rude.

And I was sad, O my true love,
For the love left unsaid:
I will sing it to the turtle-dove
That hugs her high-built bed:
I will say it to the solemn grove
And to the innocent dead.

THE MORNING-WATCH

O joys! Infinite sweetness! with what flowers,
And shoots of glory, my soul breaks, and buds!
      All the long hours
      Of night, and rest
      Through the still shrouds
      Of sleep, and clouds,
    This dew fell on my breast;
      O how it *bloods*,
And *spirits* all my earth! hark! In what rings,
And *hymning circulations* the quick world
      Awakes, and sings;
      The rising winds,
      And falling springs,
      Birds, beasts, all things
    Adore him in their kinds.
      Thus all is hurled
In sacred *hymns*, and *order*, the great *chime*
And *symphony* of nature. Prayer is
      The world in tune,
      A spirit-voice,
      And vocal joys
    Whose *echo* is heaven's bliss.
      O let me climb
When I lie down! The pious soul by night
Is like a clouded star, whose beams though said

To shed their light
Under some cloud
Yet are above,
And shine, and move
Beyond that misty shroud.
So in my bed
That curtained grave, though sleep, like ashes, hide
My lamp, and life, both shall in thee abide.

HENRY VAUGHAN (*c.* 1621–95)

A PRAYER AT MORNING

Cold, slow, silent, but returning, after so many hours.
The sight of something outside me, the day is
     breaking.
May salt, this one day, be sharp upon my tongue;
May I sleep, this one night, without waking.

WAKING IN WINTER

I can taste the tin of the sky – the real tin thing.
Winter dawn is the color of metal,
The trees stiffen into place like burnt nerves.
All night I have dreamed of destruction,
      annihilations –
An assembly-line of cut throats, and you and I
Inching off in the gray Chevrolet, drinking the green
Poison of stilled lawns, the little clapboard
      gravestones,
Noiseless, on rubber wheels, on the way to the sea
      resort.

How the balconies echoed! How the sun lit up
The skulls, the unbuckled bones facing the view!
Space! Space! The bed linen was giving out entirely.
Cot legs melted in terrible attitudes, and the nurses –
Each nurse patched her soul to a wound and
      disappeared.
The deathly guests had not been satisfied
With the rooms, or the smiles, or the beautiful rubber
      plants,
Or the sea, hushing their peeled sense like Old Mother
      Morphia.

THE WAKING

I strolled across
An open field;
The sun was out;
Heat was happy.

This way! This way!
The wren's throat shimmered,
Either to other,
The blossoms sang.

The stones sang,
The little ones did,
And flowers jumped
Like small goats.

A ragged fringe
Of daisies waved;
I wasn't alone
In a grove of apples.

Far in the wood
A nestling sighed;
The dew loosened
Its morning smells.

I came where the river
Ran over stones:
My ears knew
An early joy.

And all the waters
Of all the streams
Sang in my veins
That summer day.

THEODORE ROETHKE (1908–63)   233

THE HARBOR DAWN

Insistently through sleep – a tide of voices –
They meet you listening midway in your dream,
The long, tired sounds, fog-insulated noises:
Gongs in white surplices, beshrouded wails,
Far strum of fog horns ... signals dispersed in veils.

And then a truck will lumber past the wharves
As winch engines begin throbbing on some deck;
Or a drunken stevedore's howl and thud below
Comes echoing alley-upward through dim snow.

And if they take your sleep away sometimes
They give it back again. Soft sleeves of sound
Attend the darkling harbor, the pillowed bay;
Somewhere out there in blankness steam

Spills into steam, and wanders, washed away
– Flurried by keen fifings, eddied
Among distant chiming buoys – adrift. The sky,
Cool feathery fold, suspends, distills
This wavering slumber.... Slowly –
Immemorially the window, the half-covered chair
Ask nothing but this sheath of pallid air.

And you beside me, blessèd now while sirens
Sing to us, stealthily weave us into day –
Serenely now, before day claims our eyes
Your cool arms murmurously about me lay.
While myriad snowy hands are clustering at the
     panes –

    your hands within my hands are deeds;
    my tongue upon your throat – singing
    arms close; eyes wide, undoubtful
              dark
                drink the dawn –
    a forest shudders in your hair!

The window goes blond slowly. Frostily clears.
From Cyclopean towers across Manhattan waters
– Two – three bright window-eyes aglitter, disk
The sun, released – aloft with cold gulls hither.

The fog leans one last moment on the sill.
Under the mistletoe of dreams, a star –
As though to join us at some distant hill –
Turns in the waking west and goes to sleep.

HART CRANE (1899–1932)   235

FIRST THINGS FIRST

Woken, I lay in the arms of my own warmth and
    listened
To a storm enjoying its storminess in the winter dark
Till my ear, as it can when half-asleep or half-sober,
Set to work to unscramble that interjectory uproar,
Construing its airy vowels and watery consonants
Into a love-speech indicative of a Proper Name.

Scarcely the tongue I should have chosen, yet, as well
As harshness and clumsiness would allow, it spoke in
    your praise,
Kenning you a god-child of the Moon and the West
    Wind
With power to tame both real and imaginary monsters,
Likening your poise of being to an upland county,
Here green on purpose, there pure blue for luck.

Loud though it was, alone as it certainly found me,
It reconstructed a day of peculiar silence
When a sneeze could be heard a mile off, and had me
    walking
On a headland of lava beside you, the occasion as
    ageless
As the stare of any rose, your presence exactly
So once, so valuable, so very now.

This, moreover, at an hour when only too often
A smirking devil annoys me in beautiful English,
Predicting a world where every sacred location
Is a sand-buried site all cultured Texans do,
Misinformed and thoroughly fleeced by their guides,
And gentle hearts are extinct like Hegelian Bishops.

Grateful, I slept till a morning that would not say
How much it believed of what I said the storm had said
But quietly drew my attention to what had been done
– So many cubic metres the more in my cistern
Against a leonine summer – putting first things first:
Thousands have lived without love, not one without
     water.

ENTRANCE FROM SLEEP

To wake into the afternoon for you
Is a familiar gesture. Upon the eye,
As dawn to the shade-embroidered fountain brings
The young fern's wisdom, the first world takes shape
Where shadow and light on a white ceiling meet;
And the late garden builds its trellises
And the machinery of light begins.

To wake is to become what one first sees.
So, waking upon beaches, one is a shell,
A tide; or, afternoons in an apartment
Above a garden, levels of shade and sun
Through which you wade like eyes in tapestries
That wake only when struck by light and take
Advantage of this grace to change our sleep

Or plant an image of our wakening.
So you, with a Medici smile, becoming not
A twilight personage but the danceable gloom
And music of all shade, wake trailing song
As in an hour of hot brilliance what
Happens is a wrung memory of light
And all shade is what music we have rung.

238   JAMES MERRILL (1926–95)

WAKING IN A NEWLY BUILT HOUSE

The window, a wide pane in the bare
modern wall, is crossed by colourless
peeling trunks of the eucalyptus
recurring against raw sky-colour.

It wakes me, and my eyes rest on it,
sharpening, and seeking merely all
of what can be seen, the substantial,
where the things themselves are adequate.

So I observe them, able to see
them as they are, the neutral sections
of trunk, spare, solid, lacking at once
disconnectedness and unity.

There is a tangible remoteness
of the air about me, its clean chill
ordering every room of the hill-
top house, and convoking absences.

Calmly, perception rests on the things,
and is aware of them only in
their precise definition, their fine
lack of even potential meanings.

THOM GUNN (1929–   )   239

AUBADE

I work all day, and get half-drunk at night.
Waking at four to soundless dark, I stare.
In time the curtain-edges will grow light.
Till then I see what's really always there:
Unresting death, a whole day nearer now,
Making all thought impossible but how
And where and when I shall myself die.
Arid interrogation: yet the dread
Of dying, and being dead,
Flashes afresh to hold and horrify.

The mind blanks at the glare. Not in remorse
– The good not done, the love not given, time
Torn off unused – nor wretchedly because
An only life can take so long to climb
Clear of its wrong beginnings, and may never;
But at the total emptiness for ever,
The sure extinction that we travel to
And shall be lost in always. Not to be here,
Not to be anywhere,
And soon; nothing more terrible, nothing more true.

This is a special way of being afraid
No trick dispels. Religion used to try,
That vast moth-eaten musical brocade
Created to pretend we never die,
And specious stuff that says *No rational being*

Can fear a thing it will not feel, not seeing
That this is what we fear – no sight, no sound,
No touch or taste or smell, nothing to think with,
Nothing to love or link with,
The anaesthetic from which none come round.

And so it stays just on the edge of vision,
A small unfocused blur, a standing chill
That slows each impulse down to indecision.
Most things may never happen: this one will,
And realisation of it rages out
In furnace-fear when we are caught without
People or drink. Courage is no good:
It means not scaring others. Being brave
Lets no one off the grave.
Death is no different whined at than withstood.

Slowly light strengthens, and the room takes shape.
It stands plain as a wardrobe, what we know,
Have always known, know that we can't escape,
Yet can't accept. One side will have to go.
Meanwhile telephones crouch, getting ready to ring
In locked-up offices, and all the uncaring
Intricate rented world begins to rouse.
The sky is white as clay, with no sun.
Work has to be done.
Postmen like doctors go from house to house.

PHILIP LARKIN (1922–85)   241

TOWARDS BREAK OF DAY

Was it the double of my dream
The woman that by me lay
Dreamed, or did we halve a dream
Under the first cold gleam of day?

I thought: 'There is a waterfall
Upon Ben Bulben side
That all my childhood counted dear;
Were I to travel far and wide
I could not find a thing so dear.'
My memories had magnified
So many times childish delight.

I would have touched it like a child
But knew my finger could but have touched
Cold stone and water. I grew wild
Even accusing Heaven because
It had set down among its laws:
Nothing that we love over-much
Is ponderable to our touch.

I dreamed towards break of day,
The cold blown spray in my nostril.
But she that beside me lay
Had watched in bitterer sleep
The marvellous stag of Arthur,
That lofty white stag, leap
From mountain steep to steep.

THE SUNNE RISING

    Busie old foole, unruly Sunne,
      Why dost thou thus,
Through windowes, and through curtaines call on us?
Must to thy motions lovers seasons run?
    Sawcy pedantique wretch, goe chide
    Late schoole boyes and sowre prentices,
  Goe tell Court-huntsmen, that the King will ride,
  Call countrey ants to harvest offices;
Love, all alike, no season knowes, nor clyme,
Nor houres, dayes, moneths, which are the rags of time.

    Thy beames, so reverend, and strong
      Why shouldst thou thinke?
I could eclipse and cloud them with a winke,
But that I would not lose her sight so long:
    If her eyes have not blinded thine,
    Looke, and to morrow late, tell mee,
  Whether both the India's of spice and Myne
  Be where thou leftst them, or lie here with mee.
Aske for those Kings whom thou saw'st yesterday,
And thou shalt heare, All here in one bed lay.

    She is all States, and all Princes, I,
      Nothing else is.
Princes doe but play us, compar'd to this,

All honor's mimique; All wealth alchimie;
    Thou sunne art halfe as happy as wee,
    In that the world's contracted thus.
   Thine age askes ease, and since thy duties bee
   To warme the world, that's done in warming us.
Shine here to us, and thou art every where;
This bed thy center is, these walls, thy spheare.

SONG OF APOLLO

The sleepless Hours who watch me as I lie
    Curtained with star-enwoven tapestries
From the broad moonlight of the open sky,
    Fanning the busy dreams from my dim eyes, –
Waken me when their mother, the grey Dawn,
Tells them that dreams and that the moon is gone.

Then I arise; and climbing Heaven's blue dome,
    I walk over the mountains and the waves,
Leaving my robe upon the ocean foam;
    My footsteps pave the clouds with fire; the caves
Are filled with my bright presence, and the air
Leaves the green Earth to my embraces bare.

The sunbeams are my shafts with which I kill
    Deceit, that loves the night and fears the day;
All men who do, or even imagine ill
    Fly me; and from the glory of my ray
Good minds and open actions take new might,
Until diminished by the reign of night.

I feed the clouds, the rainbows and the flowers
    With their aethereal colours; the moon's globe
And the pure stars in their eternal bowers
    Are cinctured with my power as with a robe;

Whatever lamps on Earth or Heaven may shine
Are portions of one spirit; which is mine.

I stand at noon upon the peak of Heaven;
    Then with unwilling steps, I linger down
Into the clouds of the Atlantic even;
    For grief that I depart they weep and frown –
What look is more delightful, than the smile
With which I soothe them from the Western isle?

I am the eye with which the Universe
    Beholds itself, and knows it is divine;
All harmony of instrument and verse,
    All prophecy and medicine are mine,
All light of art or nature: – to my song
Victory and praise, in its own right, belong.

ACKNOWLEDGMENTS

Thanks are due to the following copyright holders for permission to reprint:

AUDEN, W. H.: 'Lullaby', copyright © 1972 by W. H. Auden and 'Twelve Songs: Song IV' ('Dear though the night is gone'), 'Prime' from *Horae Canonicae* and 'First Things First', copyright 1957 by W. H. Auden, from *Collected Poems* by W. H. Auden, copyright © 1976 by Edward Mendelson, William Meredith and Monroe K. Spears, Executors of the Estate of W. H. Auden. Used by permission of Random House, Inc. and Faber and Faber Ltd. BELLOC, HILAIRE: 'The Early Morning' and 'On a Sleeping Friend' by Hilaire Belloc from *Complete Verse*. Reprinted by permission of PFD on behalf of the Estate of Hilaire Belloc, copyright © 1970 by the Estate of Hilaire Belloc. BISHOP, ELIZABETH: 'Insomnia', 'Love Lies Sleeping' and 'Sunday, 4 a.m.' from *The Complete Poems: 1927–1979* by Elizabeth Bishop. Copyright © 1979, 1983 by Alice Helen Methfessel. Reprinted by permission of Farrar, Straus and Giroux, LLC. BOGAN, LOUISE: 'July Dawn' and 'Tears in Sleep' from *The Blue Estuaries* by Louise Bogan. Copyright © 1968 by Louise Bogan. Copyright renewed 1996 by Ruth Limmer. Reprinted by permission of Farrar, Straus and Giroux, LLC. CAVAFY, C. P.: 'An Old Man',